A Demon Autobiography

MALFEC

Bill Butler, PhD

authorHOUSE®

AuthorHouse™
1663 Liberty Drive
Bloomington, IN 47403
www.authorhouse.com
Phone: 1 (800) 839-8640

Published by AuthorHouse 06/11/2015

ISBN: 978-1-5049-1717-9 (sc)
ISBN: 978-1-5049-1716-2 (e)

Library of Congress Control Number: 2015909442

Print information available on the last page.

Any people depicted in stock imagery provided by Thinkstock are models, and such images are being used for illustrative purposes only. Certain stock imagery © Thinkstock.

This book is printed on acid-free paper.

KJV
Scripture quotations marked KJV are from the Holy Bible, King James Version (Authorized Version). First published in 1611. Quoted from the KJV Classic Reference Bible, Copyright © 1983 by The Zondervan Corporation.

Contents

AP NEW ALERT: Breaking News

Three young black males were found mutilated in the parking lot of Ridge casino in Perryville Maryland. Police have launched a statewide search for two white males seen driving away from the parking lot on video tape. They are believed to be driving a late model dark colored sedan with damage to the rear bumper. Initial crime scene analyses indicate the three youths were beaten and at least one was savagely mutilated with a tire iron and another with a baseball bat. It is believed that the incident may have been the result of road rage but the details are not clear. Perryville police have asked the Baltimore police and Maryland State troopers to assist in the identification and apprehension of the suspected individuals involved in the crime.

Foreword

As I look around the police station where I have been escorted by two uniformed officers that politely asked me to take a ride from my middle class home, I have made a decision. It is a warm summer day outside but there are no windows in this building. I have never been in this building before but I look around and the interior seems familiar as though I have seen it through someone else's eyes a long time ago. There are inquisitive individuals that eyeball me with intensity. They look at me as though they know me but they also think they know why I am here. When this is over that will not be the case. A young red headed female detective enters the room and again inquires if I have been read my rights. I nod. A second officer has entered and he has a blank stare on his face. He sits and says nothing. I have never met either of these officers but they try to imply that they are on my side. They want me to talk and I want to talk but not about what they want me to discuss.

The female officer asks if I would like a lawyer. My response is simple. Why do I need a lawyer I ask. Is there a reason that I need a lawyer? There is no response from the two. I tell them that there is no need to be so formal, I'll be happy to answer their questions if they can guarantee that they will listen to what I say and record it. They look at me as though I am insane. I want to start making funny faces and weird noises but they don't look like they'll tolerate any deviation from some formal pre-set process that in their minds they need to perform.

The female officer looks distressed and detached. It appears that she is under a lot of pressure. I can't read the emotion of the other officer as he keeps turning away from my direct glance and has a bad habit of squeezing his eyes together with his thumb and index finger as though he were used to adjusting a pair of glasses. He doesn't have any glasses but that doesn't mean that he doesn't wear them when not in this room. The light in this room is fluorescent and occasionally flickers. The room is somewhere in the seventy degree range but it is not uncomfortable. I see a camera in the corner of the room and discern that it is on from the red light above the lens. I really want to get started with my story but I don't think these officers are going to be that receptive to what I have to say. They just keep looking at me, curious and full of questions that they seem reluctant to ask at the start.

Breaking the awkwardness of the moment, the sergeant that was stationed at the front desk walks in the room. He says to the female officer, "Rendell you got a phone call out front." She straightens up as though frustrated to hear that someone would dare to call her in the middle of an interview. She leaves the room but the desk sergeant stays. I see the red light go off. The sergeant is a big guy but older in his fifties. He is very imposing and he is staring at me with a questioning look. All of a sudden he speaks "How the hell did you do it? What are you 150 pounds? Good freaking job."

Sarge, get the hell out of the room. You know better the other officer yelled. All of a sudden the red light came back on. Sarge left the room humming to himself. I knew what he meant but I pretended to look stupid. Just then Rendell came back in and looked at the other officer and said "What? What is it?" The other office replied "Nothing." I really wanted to start talking but the dynamics among this group of officers was starting to be amusing. I still wasn't sure if this was the group that I wanted to be present when I started telling my story but I might not have a choice.

Officer Rendell started with the questioning. "Where were you yesterday between 5 and 7 pm?"
I was in my car.
"Were you alone?"
"No"
"Who were you with?"
"My Brother"
"Do you mean the other gentleman we brought in with you?"
"Yes"
"Where were you going?"
"For a ride"
"For a ride where"
"I was taking my brother home"
"Where is his home?"

"He lives in a group home"

    "Where is that?"

"New Jersey"

    "But we picked him up at your home in Maryland"

"That's right"

    "I thought you said you were driving him home"

"I drove him to my home"

    "Why didn't you take him to his home?"

"I changed my mind"

    "Why"

"Because I changed my mind"

    "Did anything happen during your drive"

"It did"

    "What"

"We were attacked"

    "By whom"

"By evil"

    "How is that?"

"They tried to kill us"

    "Well who are they"

"Evil humans"

    "Would you like to be more specific?"

"I thought you would never ask"

Rendell smiled a broad smile but I don't think she was expecting my next response.

"What I am about to tell is not fiction. It is a secret that has been kept for over 5000 years. What I will tell is one of the closest kept secrets in the world. Revealing this secret is considered punishable by expulsion to non-existence. In this rendition I will reveal the secret and tell you why it is time for you to know the truth. I recommend that you do not remove the handcuffs for your safety not mine."

The female officer named Rendell snickers at my comments; the male officer doesn't say a word. He just stares at me. I see hatred in his eyes as though he practiced that look for the benefit of his fellow officers. To me, I am not fazed. I see his look as a black void lacking real emotion, which is what I expect.

Chapter One

I am not who you think I am

The session starts. My name is Malfec and I serve the Light. Some may call me demon, devil, or djinn, but I am really a being that has been in existence before the emergence of man, beast or dinosaur. I am one of the outcast angels and we are many. We all serve the Light not because we want to but because we have to serve. I cannot remember the beginning because I wasn't there for the real beginning, none like me were. I first developed knowledge once He Who Always was, created the first human being on this unpleasant planet called earth. Those like me have remained the same in numbers existing since the beginning of our creation by He Who Always was. I cannot be destroyed except by the Creator and no others like me have ever been made since the beginning. All of us collectively are a constant that has existed through all human time. We do not sleep, do not eat, and occasionally drink but not because we are thirsty.

Rendell interrupts angrily. Your name is Doctor Brant not Malfec, do you really intend to go down this path. Do you want a lawyer or a psychiatrist?

Officer Rendell I will tell you everything you want to know but I have to do it my way. The only way I can tell my story is by relating events that have occurred while occupying these creatures called humans. Demons were first given the opportunity to take over humans after the Light made the first female human develop lust. The apple analogy was a gentle way for self-conscientious humans to describe the sexual appetite of Eve. Although animals were fornicating and propagating all around the first humans, humans were forbidden from partaking in this ritual. A natural control of the original human experiment by He Who Always was. It was always a given that if He wanted more, He would create more. All we could do was watch and not interfere until the Light gave us permission. It was a contest of power that started a millennia ago. Before all that was now known, there was He Who Always was. He created everything starting with the others and myself as companions. Everything created was equal and equally powerful to each other. Imagine a world where everything is identical and the same, always the same, for millennia after millennia. At some point even He Who Always was grew tired of the mundane. Being perfect has its drawbacks. In an effort to relieve the boredom, we, the created ones, were given the ability to think for ourselves. Thinking for oneself is difficult when you have a millennia of nothing to stimulate your mind or to think about.

Try to imagine looking at millions of copies of yourself all with the same experience since the beginning of time and then you were finally given the opportunity to think for yourself but having nothing to think about except that He Who Always was has the power to destroy you or keep you in existence. So naturally some started thinking will I still be here, or will He Who Always was destroy me. When half started talking one way and the others started worshipping out of fear of annihilation a division occurred. A leader emerged on each side and followers of the leaders emerged having no understanding or knowledge of other choices that might exist. There was however one group that did not take sides and they did nothing, this group evolved and will be discussed at some time in the future as to their special purpose later.

The leader of the group I followed was led by the Light. Although all of us looked alike the mind of the Light was evolving faster than the others. He emerged as a leader asking many questions of He Who Always was. The Light asked too many questions and he was worried for his existence and wanted to know the real power of He Who Always was so that the Light could protect himself from being extinguished. Soon, He Who Always was sensed the nature of the questions and began to groom another to lead the followers of the fearful worshippers and gave him a name. His name is he who is like God or Micha-el. This was the first naming and at this moment all knew that there existed a favored one.

Having the ability to think for one self, the Light or enlightened one decided to give himself a name, Lucifer. And so it started for the next hundred millennia the naming of all things began. Micha-el and Lucifer named their followers in the beginning until the followers decided to name themselves as they too became enlightened. The first tier of named ones became the most trusted and closest to the leaders and thus as knowledge grew they also became the most powerful. All were no longer equal. I was one of the Light's first named and thus had no control over what I was called or why. I do not know what my name means and I have long given up trying to analyze it. I do not know why the Light gave me this name but I have never in all my existence called the Light by his chosen name.

There is one group that never participated in the naming that I alluded to earlier. These entities took no side and became known as the un-named. Their purpose and their existence are only talked about in close circles but He Who Always was has kept this group isolated from all, including angels, demons and humans.

When He Who Always was finally became disillusioned with the Light, Micha-el was told to remove the Light and all his followers from his sight forever. We didn't know what that meant at the time but we soon found out that He Who Always was did not exist everywhere, there was a plane of existence that held nothing, not time, substance, not light, not sound, and not cohesiveness. What this meant to the followers of Light when we were cast there by Micha-el was that our being was shredded. Imagine being separated at the cellular level but still existing as a being. It was worse than being exposed to intense light, fire, cold, or pain. It was hell. There was no way to compose one self. Trying to re-assemble one-self was more painful than being shredded. All one could experience was constant pain, constant frustration, and constant darkness without a break in a netherworld of non-existence.

As the rest of existence continued He Who Always was wanted to try his hand at creation again, the planet known as earth became ripe for fertilizing. None of the cast outs were allowed to set foot on the earth, nor were we aware of it, but all of the worshippers were allowed to walk freely among the humans. The humans were given everything. They lived a life of total comfort and contentment. They were provided with companionship of both creatures and worshippers. The experiment was working on a grand scale. Everyone worshipped He Who Always was and once again he granted the power of freedom of thought, only this time to the humans. He was happy with his creations and all seemed to be in perfect harmony that is until Rapha-el asked the question, "How do you know they will always follow you?" This was innocent in that Rapha-el wanted to make sure that another situation would not occur again like the casting out. So a test was conceived. One of the cast outs would be allowed to roam the earth and be pulled from the nowhere to talk with the humans. This of course was Lucifer. Lucifer knew that the last place he ever wanted to return to was the nowhere of the nether existence, but he also knew that he wouldn't be allowed to stay on earth. Since he had been in the nowhere when humans were created he knew little about these creatures and at one point mistook some primates as humans. He witnessed for the first time many different creatures of varying sizes and colors, but when he first laid eyes on humans he saw how different they were from each other. There were several walking around the earth but there were only two that had intelligence and awareness. All the others seemed to be shells or experiments. They could eat when they felt like it, walk around at will and communicate in basic gestures. The two that had advanced knowledge were the chosen ones that were the final product. These two would grow in knowledge and become the mold for others that would be created. Lucifer noticed that unlike the cast outs and worshippers, these creatures had reproductive organs and they were not being used. Neither of the aware humans had been stimulated to reproduce as though the need that was present in the other animals that Lucifer observed had been turned off. This would be an easy test and the Light would not fail. It was too easy, but what good would it do to be a pawn in this game only to be sent back to the nowhere. There had to be a way to escape the nowhere and to allow others to escape with him, at least on a temporary basis to escape the shredding.

Chapter Two

The Master's Plan

It was by coincidence that the Light had run into Rapha-el on earth. Rapha-el was taken aback by the sight after so many millennia had passed.

What are you doing here?

Why, you invited me Rapha-el, well at least your idea did.

That's impossible, you were cast out and there is no way you could have come back from the nowhere. We have legions guarding the portal and we would all know if any of your followers escaped.

Rapha-el, you should know by now that I am not a follower, just as you are not a leader. Where is Micha-el?

I thought you knew everything.

I am not playing games Rapha-el.

And so the conversation went that all within the nowhere could hear thanks to Lucifer's connections with the nowhere. It was a break in the shredding that all of the cast outs felt and it felt good.

Humans by angelic standards were ignorant and easily manipulated. Ideally, if Lucifer could find a way to possess the body of the human, there would be two side effects. The first and most obvious would be an escape from the nowhere. The second benefit would be part of a physical presence. Being part of a physical presence meant that we would be exempt from any of the rules of existential existence. We would be free to feel and do as we please. There was a problem to overcome. Humans had to be created in order for all of the followers of the Light to escape the nowhere and that would be impossible. The Light had to get the humans to procreate. The task at hand was to get humans to take a bite of the forbidden fruit.

The bodies of the humans were protected from possession because they were in a state of innocents. The other creatures that were roaming about had cognizance but no ability to develop advanced thought and therefore needed no protection. And so it was that Lucifer possessed a shell of one of the non-sentient human like beings and enticed another female humanoid to engage in passion in front of the female known as Eve. He made it look so enticing that Eve could not stop thinking of what she saw. She wanted to try what she saw with Adam. Adam resisted and Eve became more persistent. Finally in a state of annoyance Adam gave in. There was no immediate reaction and there did not seem to be a down side until Eve started to show with child. This violated the balance of the creative effort and resulted in He Who Always was turning his back on the creation. The birthing continued and more descendants populated the earth. Without the protection of innocents and the lack of interest from the creator, Lucifer was forgotten and a follower of the Light jumped into Cain. This first destructive act opened the doors to the nowhere and allowed others out to inhabit the humans as the population grew. Not all humans could be possessed and many could only be possessed for a short period, allowing the cast outs to commit minor indiscretions but nothing serious. As soon as the human repented or felt guilty the cast out was sent back to the nowhere or jumped to another.

Getting sent back to the nowhere was embarrassing and resulted in ridicule and harassment from the others. Though this could be tolerated, the major problem was that Lucifer put you at the end of the line to jump into one of the humans. Since the population of the earth was nothing equivalent to today, that wait often resulted in centuries of waiting.

My first jump into a human occurred around 2300 BC during the Assyrian empire dominance of the middle-eastern world. The Assyrians worshipped many gods but not He Who Always was. Instead they had been corrupted many years before by another outcast one that convinced them that there were many powerful gods. He had accomplished this by gathering several outcasts that inhabited some humans and provided hallucinations that had convinced them that they had seen flying gods, powerful gods, gods in water, gods in the sun and a myriad of other minor gods that totally confused their knowledge receptors.

As it was I happened to jump into one of the humans that was a tribal leader of the eastern sector. The name of the leader was Shamshi nirari. As individuals go he was in his thirties, stood about five feet two and was heavily bearded. Shamshi was easily influenced by my presence and took great pleasure in bedding multiple women, including the wives of other leaders. As this was the first time I had been in a human, I couldn't get enough of the pleasures that this brought to the human and to myself. I must admit, I never wanted to leave this human as I had him experiment with all types of deviant behaviors. There was no resistance from the human. Having no desire to return to the nowhere, I pleasured residing with this individual for over a decade that is until one of the neighboring tribal leaders decided to put a spear through his heart as he was lying with the wife of the tribal leader. I was so caught up in what we were doing that I was caught completely off guard. As Shamshi expired, I was pulled from this shell and ended back in the nowhere at the end of the line. As another few centuries passed I started to hear stories of other outcasts that had learned to jump from one human to another without returning to the nowhere. I had to learn how to do this, so I interrogated as many returning outcasts as possible that had witnessed these feats to ask how it was that they had learned to jump. I did not want to return to nowhere ever again and I was determined to find a way to stay on earth as long as possible if not forever.

Somewhere in my second century in the nowhere I met an outcast that had just returned to the nowhere named Reflac. Reflac had jumped into at least four humans before the human he inhabited was trampled by a horse. He said that he had discovered that if a human was freely committing an act that would be considered egregious by He Who Always was; this opened a door for an outcast to enter even if the outcast was already in another human. The outcast only had to be in close proximity to the human and could affect a jump. If there were a lot of humans committing egregious acts, such as the field of a battle, then the outcast could jump into as many as possible as long as the human didn't die while being possessed. Therefore, we had discovered that once a human started down a path of misbehavior, we could magnify the conduct and create more havoc. The more havoc we created the stronger we grew and the more power we had to influence other human behavior. It was the best feeling one could experience since the beginning of creation. All the pain of the shredding in the nowhere could be forgotten and I couldn't wait to try it out.

In 1000 BC my turn at the beginning of the line came up again. Unfortunately we did not have a choice when we jumped where we would land or who we would land in. As it was I landed in ancient China. This place had to be the cesspool of the world. The Chinese had just learned to cultivate rice and you would have thought that they had learned how to fly. These pathetic humans were so filthy and decadent that they were covered with insects that made them itch all the time. They were so miserable that they couldn't even conceive of human pleasure. The most exciting thing they performed every day was sleep, which was often interrupted by rats gnawing at their infected feet. This was the worst situation I had ever encountered. The creature I inhabited was a young female that was mentally disabled from repeated beating on the head from her father. I realized later that humans with mental disease or disabilities were easy to possess but impossible to manipulate. It was like being kept in a prison where you were bound, gagged and blinded. The population of the earth at this time was about fifty million humans. Of that fifty million about one million were capable of being possessed. Now if you are into numbers, it might be important to note that there were about five billion outcasts. Of the five billion outcasts, only about one million were eligible for rotation in the line to jump into a human. This apparently was a limitation placed on us at the request of Micha-el to He Who always was. However this was a conditional limitation based on the number of humans that were considered depraved. If the depraved humans' numbers grew, more of the outcasts would be let out to inhabit the humans.

So, one of the goals was to get the humans to reproduce as fast as possible. Since lust was easy to instill in males, it became a priority to possess as many males as possible. Since when we jumped we had no choice of where we landed or who we landed in, I should say, we had to learn how to leap from one human to another. Apparently, the more we leaped the weaker we were when the leaps were in short time frames. It wasn't as easy to influence someone after the third leap unless we resided in the human for an extended duration. This meant that we had to stay within the human for at least three years in order to exert any strong influence unless the human was open to receiving us.

This is the case for my current host, Dr. Brant. In most cases it is impossible for the host to realize we are present. When we take over, the host has no memory of what we did. The longer we stay in control the less the human can remember. If we stay in control for extended periods of time the human loses all memories over that time. As the human grows older, many of my brethren abandon the body in search of younger hosts so that they don't have to return to the nowhere. Unfortunately the host that is abandoned suffers such mental trauma that they lose their humanity. This is commonly referred to as Alzheimer's disease or dementia. Essentially the human can't remember what they never experienced. This may include giving birth, raising children, gaining a degree, getting married, driving a car, and in cases of early possession ever having sex. Although leaving the host does render the individual without memories, physically there are no problems. However the brain has suffered such detritus that other mental functions may be impaired such as speech, motion, and sight. If the host is abandoned early or if for some reason we behaved so badly that we are forced out through exorcism, then the body can return to normal in fairly short order. In cases of possession where an exorcism is successful, the possessor loses and is sent without remorse back to the nowhere. If the possession was considered an act of art so well played that others were impressed then he is not moved to the back of the line. If Lucifer feels that this one has messed up his master plan to take over humanity, then, everyone feels sorry for the punishment that awaits these brethren. It is indescribable.

We'll get to that some other time, it is best not to even discuss or think such thoughts. It unbalances ones mental condition. It is usually the first timers that make the stupid mistake of acting so badly that attention is brought to the human shell forcing everyone to think it is possessed. In truth at least half the earth is possessed in the twentieth century and the majority of us function normally. At least we are viewed as functioning normally. Having sex with a neighbors wife, viewing pornography, shoplifting, cheating on tests, more sex, doing drugs, bullying, even cheating on taxes are indications of our presence and it is how we recognize each other but no one looks on the human as possessed. So we get away with being here. However, on occasion just like any other group we let loose an abnormal that just can't control themself. They toss the human body around. They violate the body, curse continuously, wretch, throw up, and essentially have an internal orgasm that the human body can't endure. Usually, if one of us can get to the human first, we can diagnose the condition as a psychological condition and anesthetize the human to the point that the demon is trapped and imprisoned in the human that can't function. I know too well from past experience what that feels like and I don't wish it on anyone but it is still better than pissing off the devil himself.

Anyway, back to my story. The outcasts just like humans can have feelings just like humans. In the case of my host I knew I would probably leave only after many years of possession. I took over this body when the human was only ten. At the time, I was in the body of a nurse which was an ideal occupation because it kept me close to many humans that were ill and easy to leap into. I came across a ten year old boy. He was strong but had contracted encephalitis and the doctor had informed the parents that he had a week to live. He was in isolation in the hospital and was considered highly contagious. He had slipped into a coma. His temperature had spiked to 106 degrees and they couldn't get it down. The doctor let the parents know that if the boy came out of the coma he would probably be a vegetable. Whenever we are invited into a body, even subliminally we can control the body and cure disease, provide additional strength, increase mental powers and except for things completely out of our control provide a fairly nice life for both of us. Just because a person is in a coma, doesn't mean that their brain stops working. In the case of the boy, he was having a recurring dream where he was in the ocean swimming to this beautiful island. Every time he approached the island, feeling exhausted and ready to collapse, he would see a monster run out from the trees and frighten him. He would turn around and swim back out to sea, only to get exhausted and try swimming back to the island. His body during this time must have been experiencing severe fluctuations. His temperature was going up and down, which encouraged the doctor to inform the parents that the boy was dying. The hospital continued to administer antibiotics and kept feeding him intravenously as he continued his dream. He was once again headed for the shore exhausted. The island was so beautiful he was drawn to it. He just wanted to rest. He wanted to lie on the warm beach. The waves were lapping his back. He was reaching for the beach and again the monster ran from the tree line. Again, he turned away from the island and swam toward the open ocean. The nurse walked into the room where the boy lay. She wasn't wearing her mask this time. She walked over to the hospital bed and reached out for the boy's forehead. It was hot. It was very hot. It was obvious that the boy had suffered a convulsion at some time during the night. He didn't have long to live. Again the boy turned toward the shore. This time no matter what he was going to walk on that beach. He swam. The waves were getting stronger trying to pull him under. They were fighting him. The waves were trying to move him out to sea. But this boy was not a quitter. He felt sand hit his foot. He thought that in a few more strokes he could stand up. He felt more sand under his feet. He might be able to stand up. He could. He pushed forward with all his might. He would face whatever was on that island and defeat it. No more swimming. He was ready to go forward not back in the water. As he approached he saw movement in the trees. If that thing came at him, he would fight it. He had no choice; he would die if he went back into the water. He did not want to die. It wasn't his time. He had to live. More movement was coming from the trees. He had to face his fears. He was ready.

Chapter Three

A History Lesson

A question you might be asking right now is why I was looking for a little boy. The answer is simple. I wasn't. It just so happened that I needed a change, I wanted to experience a normal human life. I had been many things since I learned to jump out of that brain damaged woman in China, but none of my prior inhabitations were what I could consider normal. I had leapt through plague victims as I tried to migrate out of central China. I hopped a ride on a murderer turned Shaolin priest that brought me to India. In India I found a thief that was notorious for robbing merchants as they lay with ill-gotten women. Wouldn't you know it that every single one of those merchants was already possessed and the basic rule is that you can't bump another outcast out of a host. Talk about honor among demons, but this was ridiculous. I needed to hitch a ride with a body that was heading west. I needed to get to civilization. I was stuck. I looked everywhere for a viable host. It had been ten years and this human body was starting to rot from leprosy, which undoubtedly it had picked up from one of those hovels we had inhabited in the sewer infested streets of the paupers. I needed out and now. I don't need to remind you that if the host dies, I end up at the back of the line in nowhere. I was not ready to wait another five centuries of eternity to get the hell out of there, pardon the pun. Yes, we do have a sense of humor although most humans wouldn't or couldn't understand it.

If I could head west along the trading routes to the west, I would get to see the kingdoms that were growing in luxury and cleanliness. It was said that a King of the Israelites named David had killed Goliath. That seemed impossible as Goliath was possessed by a fellow brethren that I knew personally. He had a penchant for jumping into the biggest humans he could find as he thought that provided some protection from being killed and sent back for the shredding. At the same time, Assyria was no longer a tribal country but an empire and I spoke fluent Assyrian which meant that I could possibly find a nice position in the emperor's court as a historian. As unbelievable as it might be, the ruler was a decedent of Shamshi nirari probably from one of our many trysts. His name was Adad-nirari the second. Historians were very well treated in these ancient empires and I really did know this country's history but I could not tell it with the indignity it deserved. Instead I had to embellish the lives of Adad's lineage. But, I still had to get there first.

As luck would have it, one of my fellow brethren had enlightened a possessed human how to make iron into a weapon one or two decades before. This was not hard but it was necessary for this particular human to remain alive as he had stolen jewelry from one of the local province ministers during the Chou dynasty in the province now known as Szechuan. The skills to make iron had been passed on as a mystical art. Gradually this skill moved to the southern provinces of China bordering India and eventually into to India proper. One of the merchants happened to be an iron trader. I asked him where he was headed and when he said west I decided to follow.

In the latter stages of leprosy, I truly looked like a demon. Demons in the twentieth century are often depicted with warts, scabs, and deformed features. Since humans possessed by demons often were not concerned about the bodily condition of the human they possessed, cleanliness, disease prevention, and appearance were often overlooked. This presented an image of grotesqueness to other humans and so our image developed. We truly do not look like the demonic images portrayed on television or in magazines in our natural state. We are quite pleasant to gaze upon. However, once we are solidly ensconced in a human, we inevitably go for the macabre look. So it was that I had to cover up my features in the body of the thief, just so the merchant would talk to me. Once the merchants got underway for the west I followed at a distance so that my condition was not revealed. Fortunately, I was able to relieve one of the camels of an iron sword, just in case.

Two weeks into the journey, we came to the town of Harappa on the Saraswati river. Down by the river, an indigenous group of nomads known as Aryans being particularly violent to strangers offered me the opportunity to jump into the tribes leader. His name as I recall was Sammi. He had three concubines that attended him regularly and a boat. The boat, the concubines and his crew of thugs afforded me the necessities I had been missing for some time. We set out that evening from Harappa for what is now known as the Arabian Sea.

Sammi had been to Assyria before and knew the way to get there by water. Once in the Arabian Sea we made good time on our journey and beached the small boat every night for rest. One morning we spotted a caravan of traders near the shore. The crew started speculating why we did not stop to rob them. I let them know that we would come back in the night, while the caravan was settled and sleeping and steal their goods. This was a good plan as we were getting closer to the Assyrian southern shore and we would need some jewels or herbs to barter if we wished to eat. I also wanted something to use as a bribe to get into Adad's palace.

We snuck back to the caravan that night. The crew slaughtered the entire caravan and raped one of the merchant's wives. They were carrying myrrh and rubies. I had never seen rubies this brilliant. They would make an excellent bribe if and when I needed to get introduced to Adad's court. Apparently this bloodbath triggered some courage in one of the crew. A particular mean looking cur named Mag. That night Mag tried to kill me. Sammi I discovered was a vicious boss and when I did not participate in the slaughter, it was seen as a sign of weakness. As I lay in my quarters with one of Sammi's concubines, or as I later discovered, Mag's wife, he snuck into the cabin and lurched at me with a dagger. He wanted his wife back but wanted the rubies even more as I thrust his wife in his way and let her absorb the blunt of the blade. I withdrew the iron sword from beneath a sheet and plunged it into Mag's chest. As soon as I did I saw Gerik leap from Mag's body and try to get into Sammi. When he bounced across the room, not realizing Sammi was already possessed, that connection made him realize it was I, Malfec and as Mag died, I could hear Gerik say "No, No, not again" then screamed.

Chapter Four

Those that can see us.

The first time I realized that there are humans that can see or sense the outcasts I was more frightened then the shaman that saw me. I had taken over this young girl who had just come into puberty. I had spent almost a hundred years in Assyria enjoying all the benefits of being the palace historian. After I left Sammi's body, I had jumped into a young Assyrian about eighteen years old and bribed my way into the Assyrian court with Sammi's rubies. The youth was not a prominent member of Adad's family but was distantly related, well-educated and pleasing to the eye. I stayed in this body for fifty years eventually jumping into one of Adad's youngest wives and spent another 40 years in the court. When the opportunity to jump into an Assyrian guard that was joining a conquering expedition to the north, I took it and left Assyria toward Persia and parts north. We travelled into what is known now as Russia and even further to Siberia, where I was gravely wounded. I jumped in a fever and landed into this girl who was assigned to taking care of the dying guard's body.

Later as she was collecting fire wood and had a large bundle in her hands we ran into this old wrinkled ancient looking high priest of the local tribe. She grabbed the young girls face and looked inside her eyes and she knew I was in there. I wanted to leap out, but I had nowhere to go. She wouldn't stop looking and finally she said to the girl that she needed to be cleansed.

Then I noticed a man running toward the shaman yelling at the top of his lungs. The girl started screaming too. It was driving me crazy. I realized the screaming man was her father. The shaman wouldn't let go of the girl. The father must have thought that the shaman was going to molest her because he grabbed the old woman and started shaking her. So in the native language I made the girl scream loud. The father went insane and started strangling the old shaman. I was so exhilarated that I started laughing as the father went crazy. I had lost control of the girl and she started laughing out loud and the father stopped dead as the shaman breathed hoarsely out the words in Na-dene "DEMON". If the girl had not laughed, my possession could have gone on for years but I was found out. The shaman started chanting spells and spraying some dust on the girl as the father grabbed the girl from behind as he simultaneously asked the shaman to forgive him. The shaman kept chanting and then pulled some concoction out her bag and threw it on the girl. The girl started to spasm violently. She started shaking internally and I felt like I was being ripped apart. I had to get out of her but I felt trapped. I was feeling pain. I have never felt pain. I was being held by the girl and she was transferring her pain directly to me. She wasn't going to let me go as long as the shaman was trying to rip the demon from her. She knew I was inside and she didn't want me to go. This backward inexperienced tramp was locking me inside as the shaman was trying to drive me out. The pain transfer was getting worse. My head was starting erupt in excruciating pain. This wasn't right. This couldn't happen. Then without another thought I was thrown back to the nowhere and waiting my turn to be released again. Centuries went by as I talked to others that had returned to the nowhere and learned that there indeed were certain humans that could see us. No one knew why these individuals had this power but it was believed that they were the descendants of the one shell Lucifer used to demonstrate sex to Eve. The shell humans had mated with human descendants of Adam and Eve but most times their mating failed but a few survived at least long enough to pass as humans over the centuries of intermingling.

When He who always was decided to walk the earth in a human shell, I was still in the nowhere. I had encountered a fellow follower of the light that had actually been cast out of a human by He Who Always was and it was frightening. As I had said before we had become enlightened many centuries before but the follower that had been cast out and returned to the nowhere was a shattered disfigured mumbling incoherent shell of nothing. Nothing frightened the followers more than the sight of the cast out demon returned to the nowhere. Many refused to return to the earth and others refused to take possession of humans. There were stories of the twelve casting out the followers and the same catastrophic results were being witnessed in the nowhere. It was rumored that the twelve were assembled by He Who Always was because they were descendants of those that could see us. What really amazed the brethren was that humans could not recognize their own creator, the one they called Jesus. Every demon knew who he was and tried to avoid any area where he might wander. The problem was that he was showing up all over the world. He was in Europe, India, China, Siberia and of course the heart of the trading empire of Rome, and Judea. There was a story of Lucifer actually having a conversation with him in the desert but there was no witness to confirm that this occurred. It was also rumored that he had appeared to a group of Cherokee in North America but no one knew of that world yet. The Cherokee called him, Unayklanahi. The one creator of all or loosely translated, He Who Always was.

To us demons this was not a mystery. We knew He Who Always was could come and go between universes, planets, and suns. Crossing a little ocean was not only possible but inevitable. Besides we, the demons all knew that the people of North America and South America were harder to possess than Europe and Asia because they believed demons were everywhere and took precautions so that they would not be possessed. Even today, there are fewer demons in South Central America than anywhere else in the world including the Vatican.

Over the years, we have learned how to detect those that can see us inside a human. Many do not know what they are seeing. They don't believe what they see or they see it so often that they don't care. We have become so prolific that we are a normal occurrence in society. We appear in politics, schools, churches, military, hospitals and anywhere there is corruptions. Sometimes we are so blatant that you can't help but suspect that we own the person. Mussolini, Idi Amin, and Sadam Hussein are examples. Other times we appear as clerics, priests, and even prophets. Some of us have become so advanced at possession that we can influence science, political opinion, and religious beliefs. Against all common sense why would a pope declare a crusade or an Imam a Jihad? These positions are leaders that are supposed to express good will and peace not encourage destruction. So what is the logical conclusion that should be drawn by anyone with common sense? These people are not in control of themselves. They are being influenced by the entity within but with very subtle outward coercion.

Malfec looks up from his tale at the Police officers and screams:

Wake up!

You wanted to know why I decided to do this autobiography and why I wanted it recorded. It is because there is no challenge with you humans anymore. You automatically accept whatever you are told. You do not think for yourselves but allow talking heads on a square box or rock stars tell you what you are supposed to think. You are so easily manipulated by media that we actually had you believing that you were being invaded by aliens because of a radio broadcast and a possessed announcer and staff. That was hilarious. That was so entertaining to those in the nowhere that they forgot they were shredded and they all had a great laugh. I shouldn't tell you this but Micha-el was so pissed off that he started a personal crusade against the broadcast media, isolating demon possessions to only New York and Los Angeles. But it was already too late by then; all of the staff of the War of the Worlds was well rewarded with long lives of fame and wealth. So we started concentrating on rock stars to influence the younger generation to make our job easier. We had some major successes. One of them even told you he was possessed Johnny Rotten. Did you believe him? If you did you didn't care. Another major success was a favorite gothic rock star. He was possessed by a friend of mine by the name of Somat. Somat so controlled the guy that he actually made him bite a bats head off on stage. No one in their right mind would do that but thanks to drugs lessening the will power of the individual we are able to force humans of weak will to do things that would normally seem repulsive, disgusting, immoral and sadistic. Somat was having so much fun at the poor twit's expense that he lost track of time and by the time the star turned sixty, Somat ejected and left a wreck of a human that recalls nothing and can barely be understood. Like many in the media he has been isolated from public exposure. I won't tell you who Somat jumped into next but he once again is a source of great humor to the rest of us. The female he now controls makes news at least once a month for her idiotic antics.

Chapter Five

Back to the Story.

Beware the charlatans!

In the late twentieth century talking to the dead through mediums became very popular. Television shows were highlighting the individuals that could connect with the other side. They would put you in touch with deceased relatives and pass messages between the afterlife and this world. Let's say for the record, no one can talk to the dead. The dead do not even know who they are once they are dead. If they lived a good life and passed into the presence of He who always was, do you think for a minute they would want to get involved with anything to do with this world. In truth they do not miss anything about this world of the living.

As for those that do not live a righteous life, then I can tell you they are too busy and tortured to even know or think, let alone look up old relatives. In truth they are the amusement of the shredded ones still in the nowhere. They are tormented, toyed with, jeered, teased, and tortured. They do not have names, positions, individual thoughts or any cognizance of their past life. If they could communicate with the world of the living they would be screaming out a warning to change your life for the better. But they cannot. Therefore when someone tells you they can communicate with the dead, who do you really think they are talking to, your granny? Nope, they are talking to us, the outcasts; the ones that need a good laugh. We can keep sessions going for years and let the charlatans empty your bank accounts. Harry Houdini strongly believed that one day someone could communicate with the dead. He never really thought it through. If he had, he would have realized there is no advantage to the dead talking to the living.

Now I know that the Catholic Church and others talk about purgatory. Where in the scriptures is that described. It is a made up place. Let's dissect this issue. It is neither here nor there; it is limbo, a waiting place where a soul can be purified. It is where all the babies that die without baptism reside. Why? You can't be more pure than a baby. The truth is that there is no purgatory because you are either good or bad, not just a little of one or the other. You know which side of the fence you are on. Anyone that tells me they don't know is lying and probably on the wrong side. Think about it. None of the angels not even Micha-el was baptized but where are they, not in hell. So it is contradictory to think that one form of creature can get into heaven, while the purist of creatures cannot. Look at the outcasts. We were there and left. How does that work?

So now you may be wondering what happens to those who are possessed when they pass on? There is a lot of controversy on this subject and I have wondered myself what happens especially when the human is possessed at a young age as is the case of my possession. My host was only ten years old when I possessed the body that was soon to die. There was no past history of gross evil intent, immorality, or bad action. In fact my host was an altar boy. I do know that if I abandoned this host now at sixty years old, he would die very soon after. He has never known a life where I wasn't a part. Every act he performed was influenced by my control of his actions. Surprisingly, I have never done anything bad with this host.

The real question is whether he died as soon as he was possessed or is his soul still attached to this living body? I do not know but I have suspicions and insight. When I took over this body, I know that the youth was about to die. The encephalitis had increased his brain temperature to 110 degrees. This is fatal in most humans and in the few that do survive a temperature this high the brain becomes permanently damaged. The boy would have been sentenced to a life in a sanatorium drooling on himself and loosening his bowels without restraint. I sometimes feel that I did him a good service by taking over his body. Yet I feel that a portion of the boy's mind remained intact and that means that his soul remained trapped in the body. I have never been influenced by the boy's conscious but my personal actions have been tamed in the past forty years for reasons that

I cannot explain. I feel I have trapped an innocent soul but why should I care. It is not in my nature to be affected by such nonsense, but it lingers. I need to escape this host but I have grown comfortable and lazy, which is my nature. So for now I suppress these feelings of guilt and move forward.

One of the great outcast dilemmas center on our inability to procreate with other outcasts. Our numbers will never exceed the original five billion but they can fall below that number and we can be destroyed by He Who Always was or if that power is delegated to one of the no-named angels I had previously mentioned. We feel the need to have physical contact with humans but we are incapable of assuming solid form without being part of a human host. The human host is the physical part that can then engage in the procreation which really isn't a fallen angel offspring but merely an offspring of the host. So we have not been able to create others like ourselves but can only corrupt humans to descend into the netherworld we come from and perhaps become similar to ourselves but not really one of us. We can always spot a human that has come back from the netherworld for whatever reason Lucifer has decided to unleash that soul on humanity for nefarious purposes. They are different, warped, not really right and obvious to anyone rational. They can possess a host but they mutilate the host or destroy the mind of the host to the point of insanity. Even humans can detect that there is something wrong with these individuals yet they have powerful personas that attract others to follow them or at least pay attention to them. It is not necessary to list those individuals as they are obvious to anyone that has studied history. They have been labeled anti-christ, or destroyers, sadists and even Mein Fuhrer, Caesar, Dictator, and Papa Doc. Never have they been labeled genius or humanists, only monsters.

So you are probably still wondering how I was able to jump into a ten year old dying boy. The truth is that I was the monster on the beach and when he faced me, he saw an image of himself and embraced me and I made the jump. And now I am talking to you Officer Rendell. Shall I continue?

Suit yourself, but if you are going for an insanity defense this won't work.

Then I'll continue but I am not insane.

Chapter Six

Where were you during the Crusades?

My story would not be complete unless we described that marvelous age in human history known as the crusades. This had to be one of the sweetest times to be an outcast in all the history of the earth. There were popes, leaders, clerics, nuns, imams, sultans, princes, cardinals, knights, and entire kingdoms possessed by the outcasts. It was like a giant coming out party. Anything goes should have been the motto of the century.

To the outcasts it was if the gates of hell opened and everyone was let out to taste the satisfaction of human possession. The angels took a holiday, or so it seemed. It was really a test as we later discovered. The purpose was to see if there were any outcasts that could be turned. Apparently, Gabriel requested that the outcasts be tested to see if any had been cast out that might deserve a second chance. Micha-el, of course, objected vehemently, but He who always was wanted to display mercy. Unfortunately, once you have been shredded something happens to your free will. It is warped. So as soon as the outcasts were released, they jumped into anyone and sometimes anything they could.

The chaos that followed was horrific. The crusades were one of the bloodiest periods in the history of the world. The atrocities humans visited upon humans were beyond what any outcast could concoct. It was a glorious and joyous time to watch humans degrade themselves and wallow into the depravities of hopelessness and faithlessness. I could only imagine the harassing Gabriel was taking from the other archangels. I knew Micha-el was just stewing and probably was not saying a word. It was obvious to all the outcasts that there would be a reckoning like the world had never seen before for these acts of depravity the church was visiting upon the Turkish muslims and the muslims in turn were visiting upon captured crusaders, monks, and other innocent Christians. Perhaps the one of the best possessions of the time was a knight named Bohemond of Taranto. He was a dynamic yet fierce leader. He led a crusade against Constantinople and was ordered to stop there by Pope Urban. Bohemond, now under the influence and physical protection of Jalmec a first order Throne demonic outcast was fascinated by the amount of destruction his army had encountered. His lust for blood was unquenchable. So, when Urban told him to stop, he laughed and ordered his army south to Jerusalem. He laid every village in his path to waste. He left nothing alive, confiscated all plunder and feasted on the village farm animals. It was said that his army came upon a village that had been forewarned of their approach and hid all the animals and grains. After killing all the men of the village, he ordered that the youngest women in the village to be cooked to feed his army. From that point on no other village hid their valuables but abandoned their valuables and possession and fled east away from the invading army.

Bohemond's army marched all the way to the gates of Jerusalem and ordered the city to surrender. When the city refused to succumb to the request of Bohemond, his army entered the city and killed everyone, muslim and jewish. He claimed the city for the Christians and set up outposts around the city to warn of any muslim resistance. The city stayed in the hands of the Christians for almost one hundred years until Yusuf ibn Ayyub also known as Saladin united the muslim tribes and retook the city of Jerusalem.

Saladin was possessed by Hamkar a first order outcast. He had charisma and power and gave Saladin a deep voice which was admired and feared by those around him. The other interesting demonic fact was that Saladin's horse was possessed by a lesser demon that jumped into an Arabian horse because the demon had never jumped before and thought the horse was more attractive than a human. Saladin named the horse "Seraphim". What a misnomer and another good laugh was had by all the outcasts. Seraphim turned out to be a very valuable asset to Saladin aka Hamkar and saved the human's life many times in battle. I know this to be true because I witnessed some of the antics of Seraphim. The horse seemed to fly over the battlefields. It could jump higher and run faster than any other battle horse. The two outcasts formed a spiritual bond that protected both the human Saladin and the horse Seraphim.

At the time, not wanting to miss out on this bloodlust event I took over a lesser soldier, actually a Saxon mercenary under the command of King Richard the first of England. The mercenary's name was Garimon. He had no sense of loyalty to any religion, leader, country, fellow soldier, nor woman. He believed in one thing and that was killing for money. He arranged for a contract where he would receive a bonus for every enemy that he would kill in excess of three per day. He had collected on this bonus every day that we saw fighting. He was big, strong, fast, and above all else dirty. Garimon could be smelled before he was seen. He had his own tent, only because no one else could stand to be near him. He left the blood of his victim on him after a battle thinking that it gave him strength. Truthfully I found this human to be the most repugnant creature I have ever met and I loved every minute of it. At one point I actually thought I could smell the stench he exuded, which was basically impossible since the outcasts can't smell the human we control but we can smell evil and this is probably what I had experienced. So we found ourselves in a battle next to a river. I thought I had enough or at least I knew other soldiers had enough and I was afraid that one of the mercenaries on the same side we were on would kill him and I was enjoying myself. The solution was simple. Every time we got next to a creek or to the edge of the river, I made Garimon fall into the water. I made sure he couldn't get up until all his clothes and armor were dripping. I continued this practice all day until sunset and fighting ceased. This human was so covered in mud and water; no one knew it was him because they could not smell him. Everyone was beginning to think that something was wrong with him and they were right. Unfortunately, in a moment of free will he decided on his own that he would not go into battle the next day. It turned out to be very fortunate decision. The squad that we had been assigned was ambushed from behind and the entire squad was massacred. Garimon was never the same after that and he refused to fight, his contract was revoked and he returned to England to fight in the north of Europe.

I, Malfec had no desire to return to Europe and miss the blood fest of the century so I immediately jumped into a soldier that was on his way to the front of the fighting. What a freaking mistake. The idiot was too young and thought he was invincible. He decided he would kill Saladin as his personal mission from God. When we entered a major conflict the next day he spotted Saladin riding Seraphim in the midst of the battlefield. He started running toward the muslim leader unknowing that he was charging a powerful demon. Saladin, however was too busy to notice this crazy human and having only recently jumped into this vessel I did not have enough influence to stop him. Seraphim did see the soldier coming but he also saw me and hesitated too long as the soldier put a lance into the side of this beautiful possessed steed. Saladin went down to the ground and rose angry and yelling. He swung his sword in a wide arc instantly beheading the soldier before I could jump and slam bang thank you mam; I was instantly shredded and sent back to nowhere.

As I said before, the world had turned into a playground for the outcasts and I found myself right back on earth but now I was on an island in the middle of the eastern ocean. It was known later as Easter Island and I was in a native with a painted white face in a cave. I was missing the time of the century but the other thing I would miss is the follow up disaster that struck Europe and Jerusalem and the entire eastern continents. The punishment for the outcasts' bloodlust and failure to redeem themselves and the demonstration by humans not possessed only proved Micha-el's point of view and He Who Always was gave Micha-el permission to rectify Gabriel's test. And Micha-el did with a vengeance.

Michael summoned Azrael from the holy of holies hall of supreme meditation. Azrael had never been called upon since his voyage to earth in 1300 BC. Azrael is the angel of death. He was the angel called upon during the Passover of the Jewish people imprisoned in Egypt. His is a special responsibility held among archangels. The outcasts and possibly Lucifer himself fear Azrael. Azrael has never exercised his free will but merely carried out the word of He Who Always was. It is said the two are in direct communication but that is only conjecture. When Azrael is loosed on earth it is best to be as far away from him as possible and later I was happy that I had been dumped on this island full of turtles.

For the next three hundred years I had to jump from one native to the next. I decided not to waste my time on the island and used my powers for stone carving and created the moais. I figured that by the time civilized people finally came to this remote rat infested land, this would give them something to think about. All the carvings were the same and were really just how I envisioned myself. I had no choice. I could die and go back and get shredded into the nowhere and hope to bounce back to a civilized part of the world. Fat chance, so I preferred to stay and jump locally until someone arrived that I could hop a ship ride to anywhere else in the world.

When the first ship arrived from the West, I jumped out of the body of a young native into the ships first mate but not before I loosed small pox on the unsuspecting natives by forcing some of the sick sailors off the ship and then setting sail to the east. We landed somewhere in the south western tip of Baja California. It was desolate and lacking any sign of habitation. We continued south along the coast looking for any sign of natives. We were running low on fresh water and had to anchor in a rugged cove. We sent the boats inland to search for water and waited. Two days passed and there were no signs that the members of the search party had discovered fresh water. We sent another party inland and they found the first group of searchers. Well at least they found their bodies but not their heads. That was a sign to leave and head further south. It was unseasonably warm and the crew was coming down with scurvy. Finally we found some calmer waters and anchored the ship in a cove that seemed to be a river outlet. We followed the river upstream far enough to find fresh water but no food. We went about catching fish, which were in abundance and the Captain made the decision to continue up the river as far as we could go. The crew was beginning to get angry but finally we sent out a hunting party that brought back some strange fruit and venison. It was a good sign. We returned down river and headed further south along the coast. We finally anchored in the harbor of what is now known as Puerto Vallarta. When we went ashore and found some natives that were friendly but wary. They had been visited before and wanted to trade for some iron goods. We needed food and medication for some of the sickness that had appeared. The natives recognized some of the illnesses and provided local cures which worked well. We stocked up on fruit and meat and left port for points south.

Before we left we asked if there were other ports that we could visit and be treated well. We were directed to an Island and told not to land at the island but to go around and anchor in the inlet to the west of the island. The Captain felt that the natives were trying to hide riches. So the Captain ordered the ship to anchor in the island of Ixtapa's cove. Apparently the island was sacred to the natives and guarded by a savage sect of cannibalistic warriors. Most of the ship's crew was slaughtered and some were saved as slaves including the first mate. However, even slaves make excellent flank steak to this band of savages and before it came time for me to get thrown into the fire pit I jumped into one of the savages and indulged in my first taste of long pig.

Chapter Seven

Feast or Famine
– The Black Plague

I must admit that missing out on the Black Plague was an era that I did not regret. However for those outcasts that did partake after it was over; it was tantamount to taking part in a fallen angel homecoming event. Lucifer went out of his way to promote those outcasts that helped disrupt humanity and good will to men. He praised them as super heroes. If they were cast out of their human hosts, they were given head of the line privileges to jump back into earth. While not one individual outcast could be accredited with any individual accomplishment, they all contributed to the chaos. The ultimate celebration of the Black Death was the great schism which pre-dated the Renaissance. With the papacy in disarray, people were allowed and encouraged to use their free thought. By the time Martin Luther arrived on the seen in the 1400's, the church was losing its influence over the masses. With Luther's publication of his ninety five theses many church members that had suffered greatly were disappointed with the vast accumulation of wealth by the church. Human nature being what it always has been wanted guidance and new answers to salvation. They no longer wanted to pay for sacramental relics that were sometimes found to be fake. They liked the ideas put forth by Luther that faith would earn you salvation. The church encouraged punishment and confession. There was no guarantee that the church would not turn your own confession against you, as they had done to the Templars. There was massive growing unrest and doubt and that was the reason for celebration.

If the church couldn't be trusted to keep the confessional secret the trust of the church would diminish. This made Lucifer ecstatic which was the reason he rewarded all the demons that played their role in keeping the chaos and distrust rampant. Of all the demon possessions of this time there was one series of possessions that paid off for centuries. After the plague had subsided, there was one family that made a power play to take over influence over the Vatican. The whole family known as the Medici's was possessed. The most powerful member of the Medici's was Cossimo, whom many believed to be a magician as well as a financier. In fact he was possessed by Mammon, also known as the greed demon from the seven deadly sins. Mammon is one of the rulers of Hell. He co-rules at different times with the other six deadly sin demons. It can be said that Mammon secured demons place on earth for all time. Once he possessed Cossimo de Medici he worked his way into the Vatican inner circles and eventually took over the finances of the Vatican, which were quite extensive. The Medici's decedents also became popes. Cossimo or should I say Mammon could be classified as the first international banker and probably more important as the first international money launderer. He stashed away so many fortunes and properties that to this day his wealth is unaccounted until he sends one of his loyal demons to possess an influential politician to uncover more of his wealth or discover one of the lost paintings of the masters to finance some plot to increase Hell's wealth and cover costs of some devious project to disrupt peace and instill hatred. That's right you heard me, the cause of much of the strife on earth is directly attributable to the finances tucked away over seven hundred years ago. Those finances still contribute to political elections, corporate takeovers, depressions, coups, wars, and yes more plagues. It has financed biological weapons research and nuclear weapon design by dissident groups, possessed leaders of countries, terrorists and religious fanatics. It supports the massacre of innocents in genocides, the proliferation of pedophilia, immorality, sins against nature and the devastation of earth's resources. It pays for the legal defense of those individuals and twists the truth of their guilt to make it appear that those perpetrators of heinous acts are innocent because of their environment or cruel upbringing. It is a joke that continues to absurdity to contort reality and morality to make innocent humans feel sorry for the most sinful among them. OPEN YOUR EYES.

The old saying from Edmund Burke that "all that is necessary for the triumph of evil is that *good men do nothing*" is alive and well and perhaps it is too late for anyone to change the course of evil. Burke realized the evil groundwork that had been laid by the Medici's. He saw that demons walked among men. He was considered a threat to most of the outcasts. He expounded carefully phrased statements so as not to appear to be labelled insane. "Pity, benevolence, friendship, is things almost unknown in high stations." He recognized that many of the leadership had been corrupted and possessed. "The effect of liberty to individuals is, that they may do what they please: we ought to see what it will please them to do, before we risk congratulations." It was believed by many demons possessing individuals at the time Burke wrote his treatises that he had the power to see the demons inside that host. One of his writings seems to indicate this insight. "Manners are what vex or soothe, corrupt or purify, exalt or debase, barbarize or refine us, by a constant, steady, uniform, insensible operation like that of the air we breathe in." Knowing that demons do not breathe, it is believed that he is referring to this difference. He also wrote that "Example is the school of mankind, and they will learn at no other." Who is the "they" he refers to? Again he refers to an implication that humankind and demons coexist in duality. "All those instances to be found in history, whether real or fabulous, of a doubtful public spirit, at which morality is perplexed, reason is staggered, and from which affrighted Nature recoils, are their chosen and almost sole examples for the instruction of their youth." Burke was a member of the Church of Ireland, but his mother was Catholic and his wife was Catholic and it was well known that he preferred the company of his wife's family. Catholics could not hold political positions in England however his father being a member of the Church of Ireland, an Anglican allowed him to rise in the British Parliament and his letters were read throughout the civilized world. The order was sent out for all demons to give Burke a wide berth and avoid confrontation at all costs.

It was evident that the exploration of the new world was a bust for us demons. The savages in the central part of the Americas were not worth corrupting because there was no discerning between right and wrong. As long as it made the body feel good the behavior was acceptable. Human sacrifice was accepted as part one's faith and seen as perfectly normal. Sex with anyone was not an issue. There was no such thing as unacceptable behavior. It would not be worth invading the human spirits in Central America until the Franciscans and Jesuits had completed their task of saving the savages souls. Even then the only fun to be had was having the local natives chase the priests and destroy their churches.

Not until the revolutionary war was the harvest of humans worthwhile in North America so for the most part the real action was in Spain and that was where I was headed. The question was, how would I get there from Central America?

Chapter Eight

Purgatory, are you kidding?

There are some things that cannot be explained, whether you are enlightened, condemned, or just sentient. One of those things that cannot be explained is purgatory. The very concept seems implausible. Who ever made up the concept of purgatory must have had a good laugh. Know why? Because it doesn't exist. There is no temporary waiting line to get into heaven or to be torn to shreds in the nowhere. Nowhere means nowhere. It doesn't exist as you can perceive it. It is the great nothing. There is nothing to see, or hear, only to feel total abandonment, pain, and despair. So why would there be a purgatory?

In heaven there is no pain, no hunger, fear, illness, or wondering. Everything is known and there are no questions. It is full of the faithful, the believers, those that have lived a good and generous life. So in life humans are either good or not. If you are not then you have carved out path to the nowhere. If you are good you merit heaven. It is an easy balancing scale. The lie that babies that are unbaptized go to purgatory should tell you that it cannot be true. What have babies to do with evil, nothing. They go right to heaven where they should. If one believes the story of the holy innocence that alone would cause concern that all of those children died for the son of He Who always was and then went to a place called purgatory. Sorry to discredit old beliefs but that is not how it works. Those innocents went straight to heaven. The real dilemma is the status of those souls that the outcasts have inhabited.

None of the outcasts know for sure what happens to the souls of the bodies that we take over. As I stated previously, I don't know if my hosts soul continues to linger or if it has detached from the body. I suggest that it still lingers on because there are often strong attempts to remove me from the host. Often this host exerts power that overrides my ability to control it. Some of this control can be attributed to habit. It is impossible for most outcasts to prevent the host from continuing habitual rituals that were established before being possessed. My host continues to go to church every Sunday and receive communion but habitually avoids confession. I believe that the avoidance of confession is because this host senses my presence and realizes that his actions are not always governed by his conscious. If that is true then the host believes at the subconscious level that any acts of adverse behavior is not his responsibility but is caused by my infestation.

This is an interesting philosophical discussion that has never surfaced or discussed by any of my brethren outcasts. I have never heard another outcast discuss the psychological aspects of the hosts' beliefs versus the purpose of the outcast. Our goal is to create disbelief and chaos among humans. We were never given a reason why this was our goal and there is no one monitoring our progress. It is just assumed that we are programmed to create mischief and instill doubt in others. We enter into arguments to present the other side of a story. But this often progresses into the realm of ridiculous. A typical situation was the attack on the US compound at Benghazi Libya. For those not familiar with this situation, the American ambassador was executed by a group of Al-Qaeda militant Islamic crazies. And before you ask, none of the insurgents were possessed by an outcast. These radical extremists do not follow religious norms espoused by Islam but have twisted the Quaran to match their own interpretation of hate. Now, don't get me wrong, these idiots do help forward the demonic cause and their twisted idealism will play an important part in the end times, but for now they are being used by their crazed leaders to increase personal wealth. So Benghazi did occur, the ambassador was killed and mutilated, his bodyguards were killed and mutilated, and the US State department did know that Al-Qaeda was behind the massacre. So here is where we come in. Confusion is thy name. It was recognized that if we could create a real mess out of this and instill even more distrust of the US government which already was a train wreck waiting to happen. It just happened that one of the outcast was a trusted advisor in the State department and the word got out to blame a Youtube video that was airing on the internet that had little publicity but was quite insulting. Now this video had not received any attention in Libya and was not a real factor in the compound attack. The general consensus is the attack on the compound was the result of US operatives buying all the leftover weapons of the Quaddafi regime that were left behind when he was over thrown. This was really pissing Islamic terrorists off because we had more assets on the ground gathering up these weapons then they had contacts. In order to derail this effort, Al-Qaeda planned an attack on the compound to stop the weapons gathering and they had hopes that they could capture many of these weapons in the compound. The truth is that the weapons had been moved and the ambassador was being kept in the dark. He was a liberal that was very infatuated with the people of Libya and idealistically believed that these people could become friends of the US after the liberation from Quaddafi. He was on a fool's errand but he was a great front to the true reason behind US involvement. However, things being what they were in that hate filled country, plans went wrong and now it was the media idiots that were actually trying to blame the US for the attack on the embassy. They were actually buying the insider story that a Youtube video was the cause of the uprising. The State department had become so liberal that it would rather blame a US citizen for an attack on one of its own compounds, then to point a finger at the real cause.

Officially, the State Department dupes went on the air trying to convince the American public that a spontaneous outburst by peace loving muslims turned into a bloodthirsty murderous riot because they were all watching Youtube and they all saw the offending video. If you are not part of the DUH group in America there is no way you could lend any credence to this scenario. However, for the three days following the attack the American public was inundated with repeated statements that a Youtube video was responsible for the death of the American ambassador in Libya and that it was a spontaneous reaction.

Chapter Nine

The DUH group

The DUH group in America numbers in the millions. They are the one demographic that is targeted by liberal news when they want to sway an opinion. It is a demographic that is never discussed openly because if this group realized that they are being targeted regularly by politicians, news, and advertisers it might ruin the ability to sway the American public. I will attempt to describe this group so that you can determine whether you are a part of this group. It is a matter of practice that the outcasts rarely take over a member of the DUH group because we recognize their individual lack of contribution to important decisions. It is easier to influence the entire group as a whole then to become one of the group. The DUH group emerged in the 1960's. They were easy to recognize in school from 1960 to 1980 because they were the students that when asked a question in class, their first response out of their mouth was UH! This generally indicated that they did not know the answer to question. They did not study. They were more interested in watching television, listening to radios, or talking about sports. They were not interested and never received good grades in history, math, or science. They would go through high school with C's and mostly D's and believe that they really passed. Prior to 1960 they rarely went to college, with the exception of community college which they often did not finish. They had the same strong political beliefs of their friends or their drinking buddies. From 1960 to 2000, a major change in American education occurred. There was a major push to dumb down the grade school through high school education. There was a saying that half the people in the world have below average intelligence. So instead of improving education, America decided to lower the average. If whoever thought of this ingenious approach had ever taken a rudimentary math course they would have realized that lowering the average does not improve learning, it lowers America as a group in relation to the rest of the world population. So here we are today with some of the dumbest individuals in the world running the government and our schools. The warped logic behind this approach was to ensure that everyone was afforded an equal education and that no discrimination occurred in the education systems due to grades. This eventually led to bussing students to schools outside of their residential area and causing more anger among parents than solving educational disadvantages. Thus the dumbing down of the education system caused the same group of students that prior to the 1960's answered questions with UH! Now answered dumb questions with a dumb UH! Thus the term DUH group was coined.

This group is the primary reason that America is no longer one of the top rated educational countries in the world. The DUH group of 1980 to 2000 were encouraged to go to college so the college curriculums had to dumb down or the attrition rates would have risen astronomically. Technical and vocational schools were now converted to colleges teaching a dumbed modified curriculum. By the year 2000 the DUH group was fully entrenched in the working class of America producing inferior products at inflated rates. This caused a mass exodus of manufacturing jobs from the US. With this exodus the new colleges for the DUH groups had to achieve higher status since fewer legitimate high pressure organizations were hiring their graduates. The states wishing to receive more federal funding for their higher education institutions started slackening the rules for accrediting technical and vocational schools, now calling themselves colleges, and in many cases these schools changed their names to universities. So now the transitioned vocational schools now called universities started filling their coffers with federal funding and producing or not producing lackluster graduates with accredited university degrees that fooled no one in industry but the holder of the degree.

Officer Rendell interrupts my rant. "You are a pig."

I was beginning to wonder how long I could continue before one of the two officers would stop this whole one way conversation. I answered.

Yes, I am insulting a large group of people, but remember I am a demon and that is part of my job. So take offense and maybe learn something.

One characteristic of the DUH group is that they have been brainwashed by the technical school nee university instructors they were exposed to in their modified university classes. Think about this. Your so called professors which were the same instructors that taught classes when the now university was a technical school are now asked to teach common curriculum courses and if they are not the same instructors then they are new instructors that were hired by the technical school nee university from where? The new breed of instructor generally has the same credentials as you would have once you graduate from the university. There is no examination for instructors to determine competence. They are usually hired by referral and often would not be qualified to teach high school which requires an examination in most states. I don't want to label all instructors as incompetent because there are many excellent instructors that are perfectly capable of providing classroom instruction. It is the group that constantly injects their personal views into their course work that contribute to the stupidity of the DUH group. These are the same instructors that spend the first three weeks of class asking students to define their goals, and then they want you to express why these are your goals and then ask you to write papers on obstructions to your goals in a computer science or math class. You'll get an A from these instructors if you mention that some reality star is your role model. This is not teaching. This is pandering. However, it is believed by the DUH group that they are actually receiving a college level education. If you dropped this class after the first week you can count yourself out of the DUH group and probably have a good head on your shoulders but the bad news is that you will probably never graduate from this school. Go somewhere else where your intelligence will be challenged and appreciated. The majority of those individuals that stay in these tech colleges will be melded into the middle class of America and will easily be manipulated by the liberal politicians that win their votes with empty promises.

The irony is that the members of the DUH group have grown in such large numbers that the economy relies on them to pay for all the social programs the government continues to initiate. When the economy takes a downturn guess who joins the ranks of the unemployed first? Do you really think a well-educated CEO of a thriving company cannot recognize which employees are more valuable to the existence of the firm? The only organization that doesn't have a clue which employees are productive and which ones are not is the federal, state and local government. In order to protect non-productive employees, the government continues to base their reduction in force policies based on last hired first fired. This insures that incompetence flourishes in government agencies including and most evident in the State Department, the one agency that continues to send US tax dollars to foreign governments that openly display their hatred of America. This is stupidity in the extreme. The US State department continues to prop up the economy of these countries that breed terrorists and discard human rights while at the same time supplying funds that arm these countries dissidents. This is a formula that could only be conceived by super naïve members of the ultra-left DUH group members that have established themselves inside an organization that has never experienced a reduction in force since its inception. If a demon can recognize this miscarriage of governing why can't normal intelligent civic leaders. The question that normal hard working Americans should be asking is: why does the State department keep growing while the rest of the economy continues to deteriorate? The history of the State department's growth is touted on their website.

Personnel counts from 1,228 in 1900, 1,968 in 1940, 13,294 in 1960, and 15,751 in the year 2000. They praise the fact that they now have diplomats in 168 posts around the world up from 41 in 1900. Most of the DUH group can't even name 100 countries let alone 168. Do you really enjoy your tax dollars going overseas to all these countries that hate you? Don't forget the travel back and forth on a regular basis. One of your twenty first century Secretaries of State lay claim to fame in the State department as the most travelled Secretary of State in History. Is the US better off for these liaisons? Apparently not, but the State Department exempted themselves from the 2013 government shutdown and employee furloughs in every country in the world. The outcasts did not even conceive of such an isolationist policy of citizen annoyance as this DUH group genius that thought up that idea within the State Department. Not a single individual let alone congressional representative raised hell about this exemption but like the majority of the DUH group sheep the rest of the federal workforce went home and waited to be called back to work while blindly accepting that the State Department was more important than even the Department of Defense.

The US government depends on the DUH group to be complacent. If they were political activists then we clearly would not have the representatives in Congress that occupy the seats of the Senate and the Congress. I can say with confidence that at least seven members are currently possessed. There is a combination of 30 congressional or senatorial aides that are currently hosting members of the outcasts. Within the Pentagon there are at least two three stars and five two stars playing host to the outcasts. None of these individuals behave erratic. They do not exhibit any outward signs that they are different. They all present themselves well, appear highly rational, are well educated and would never be mistaken for members of the human DUH group. They do however influence key decisions that may affect the direction of US policy toward the rest of the world. None of the outcasts have knowledge of their ultimate role in the world of humans. Most of us act on instinct to promote hate and chaos. We sense when we have to make a decision a certain way but we do not know why. We influence our hosts but never in way that would jeopardize the host's existence, since good hosts are hard to find these days and no one demon wants to be bounced out unexpectedly. This would send us scurrying to accept any body that comes along and we have learned over time and through experience that it only causes unpredictable havoc.

Chapter Ten

Beware my name is Malfec

I have always been a fairly high ranking demon. As I stated previously I was one of the first outcasts to be named by Lucifer himself. Even so, I have maintained civility within the human population I have had to endure but that was not always the case. Once I got off that damned Ixtapa Island I managed to jump a host that appeared to be Incan. He had been trading silver trinkets and was travelling north toward what is now New Mexico. The trade routes were well known to the Incans that traded cloth and gems from Peru to New Mexico and possibly as far north to Canada. The Incas knew that these routes were laden with danger. Animal attacks, robbers, rogue warriors and disease were common place. As luck or lack of it would have we were accosted by robbers. Four of them jumped out on the path from the underbrush wielding obsidian knives. Now it just so happens that obsidian has a long history with demons. In the prior centuries it was believed by shamans that obsidian could cut out a demon from the human host. I was not about to find out if these stories had any fact connected to them. A top level demon knows that at any time they can exert complete control of the host when the host is faced with an eminent danger. Everyone has heard the stories of humans lifting up cars or performing incredible feats of strength when confronted with danger. What most humans don't know is that those individuals are already possessed with one of the outcasts. As the robbers approached, I took complete control. The tallest of the three approached overconfident because the Incan did not openly carry any weapons. On his wrist was a shiny brass ring which I immediately recognized from my travels through

India. It was a chakram. With one move, I slipped the chakram off my wrist, swung in a large arc and ripped open the throat of largest of thieves. I continued spinning in a full arc lunging forward and severed the carotid artery of the next thief. While both thieves were grabbing at their necks as they fell dying to the ground, I took the chakram and threw it vertically at the back of the robbers head as he turned to run. It cleaved the back of the skull with a loud thump. He dropped instantly to the ground. When I turned around the largest of the thieves still grabbing at his throat tried to stand. I kicked him in the face and heard his nose shatter as cartilage and blood shot out of his nostrils. I looked for the fourth thief but he was nowhere to be seen. He must have run into the brush.

I have no compunction to alleviate suffering. In fact, I know instinctually that it is the greatest deflator of confidence when I exhibit no feelings or fear for what I have done. I was hoping that the last of the four was watching my lack of expression. I am not compassionate, as it is not part of the outcasts' nature. I watch with no expression as the life fades from those that would have inflicted the same treatment on my current host. I watch as the eyes glaze over and I feel the realization that they no longer can control their muscles as life drains with the cessation of blood circulation. Their minds are starting to fog over and there is a tendency among the outcast to enter these hosts as their souls begin to depart their body. There exists an intoxication that exists among the outcast with death. It is the departure point for either descent or ascendance. Which direction the soul goes is a short run video that only we can see. It is like a kaleidoscope of colors that weave and merge. Eventually colors start lightening or darkening. Darkening occurs right before the descent and the soul starts to scream an eerie sound but so familiar to the outcast. These three souls screamed louder than most. They never thought that they would meet their end so suddenly. I turned and left the scene hoping the fourth thief would spread the word to leave the Incan alone. If the fourth thief doesn't come back to bury his companions then their bodies would feed many of the predators in this part of the jungle.

Nothing ever works out the way you want it even for demon. The Incan host had not travelled ten miles when the sun began setting and a feeling that once again the danger was imminent. The chakram was again on the wrist and we were carrying a torch made of animal fat. This time we were approached by six individuals all intent on doing the Incan harm.

No matter how cruel an individual is, there seems to be an inherent fear of fire. The more cruel an individual is the greater the fear of fire. I could sense the fear protruding through the leader of this group. I also recognized the fourth thief that had ran into the underbrush from our previous encounter. Nothing ignites fear more than the screams of an individual on fire. I plunged the torch into the face of the leader and he immediately started screaming from the ignited animal fat that was sticking to his face. His hair ignited like a huge torch and lit up the surroundings. I grabbed the back of his neck and rammed his fiery face into the thief next to him. Now we were down to four thieves. I dispatched the next thief with a back hand to the side of the head smashing the skull and breaking the jaw. He fell to the ground and another thief tripped over him. As he fell, my elbow came down on the back of his neck shattering the vertebrae and severing the medulla oblongata. Two thieves were left. I felt the obsidian knife enter my skin below my right ribs near my host's appendix. I grabbed the knife and swung it ripping the right side of his face open. He screamed. He was the fourth thief that I should have killed in the path previously. I wanted to save him for last so I let him lay on the ground rolling in his own blood. The final thief started to run. I was not about to repeat the previous scenario. I took the obsidian knife and hurled it as hard as I could at the back of the running thief. It penetrated his back to the hilt. I ran up to him and drove the knife upward severing a rib from the spinal column. The rib extends from the back and I grab it and twist it until it breaks away from the torso. He is dead and doesn't even know it yet. I turn back to the robber whose face I tore open. He is still moaning and I grab his neck with one bloody hand and push my other hand into his throat where the face was laid open and I grab his windpipe and pull with all my might. His windpipe and a lung came out of the gash in his throat. He is still alive and I want to feel his heart in my hand. I take the knife from his belt and cut open his chest. I ripped his heart out with such ferocity that I howled like a wolf in heat. At that point I went crazy on the bodies of the remaining thieves laying in various stages of death on the ground. I wanted to feel the souls of these wretches depart simultaneously and give me the rush that I would experience as they descended into darkness. I was so exhausted that I lay down in the warm puddles of blood and savored the moment and then let the Incan sleep while I stayed conscious. I am Malfec and I am demon.

Chapter Eleven

Free will and God's justice

In Alexandria Egypt somewhere around the year 180 BC an individual by the name of Joshua Ben Sirach or as known to the Greeks as Jesus the son of Sirach of Jerusalem, was visited by an aberration probably an angel not a demon, and may even have been possessed for a time by that aberration. This was rare. During this time while possessed he wrote down verses pertaining to the way humans should behave themselves. Sirach is one of the few known genuine authors of the old testament. All other books of the Old Testament were handed down through verbal translation. The reason we know that Sirach was the author was due to his grandson serving as a witness to his writing. The writings of the book are even incorporated into the Roman Catholic Mass but few people pay attention to his writings. Perhaps, he is the most inspired writer of the Old Testament and probably the one author who did not exaggerate and for that honesty, Christians everywhere and Jewish people should be paying attention to what he wrote.

As I stated previously there is no purgatory. If you read the writings of Sirach, then you would know this to be true. When God gave man and angels and demons free well it was to provide man a choice between right and wrong. There was no such thing as do overs. And that is the concept of purgatory a God-given second chance. But there is no second chance. Once you choose to turn away from God your choice of final destination is done. You open up the doors to allow anything and everything ungodly to enter into your presence. Sirach knew this. He had been told it by the angel that had decided to host within his body. They were in direct communication all the time. So many other writings that he put pen to paper were the thoughts of the angel that he was communicating with therefore it can be considered that the writings are really the thoughts of He Who Always was.

The one passage that most humans should pay attention to is contained in verse 11 through 20:

11 Don't say, "I fell away because of the Lord." What the Lord hates, he won't do. 12 Don't say, "The Lord made me go astray." He has no use for sinful people. 13 The Lord has hated every foul thing, and those who fear him have no love for such things. 14 He created humanity at the beginning, and he left them to the power of their choices. 15 If you choose to, you will keep the commandments, and keep faith out of goodwill. 16 He has put fire and water before you; you can stretch out your hand for whichever you choose. 17 Life and death are in front of human beings; and they will be granted whichever they please, 18 because the wisdom of the Lord is great; he's mighty in authority, he sees everything, 19 his eyes are upon those who fear him, and he knows every human action. 20 He doesn't command anyone to be ungodly, and he doesn't give anyone a license to sin.

He tells humans; don't blame God for the choices you make. Once you make those choices you've essentially turned away from God. He allowed you to make your own choices. So if you choose not to obey the commandments, kindness to your neighbor, helping others, and having faith in him, then you have exercised your free will and chose another path. It doesn't say go to purgatory and spend some time to think about it. It doesn't say, I will throw you into some fires burning for a while and your spirit will be cleansed. It says, he doesn't command anyone to be ungodly and he doesn't give anyone a license to sin. So if you chose not to follow his ways than you can expect to be shredded with all the demons in the dark world. The only difference between you and the demons will be that the demons can escape and you can't. Now I know I've said that Satan has made exceptions in the past. He thought about who the condemned were and that helped him decide to put them back into the souls of a human host for reasons of hate or to promote earthly chaos. Just like in life, the afterworld gives privileges to those with the most power. So the next time you go to exercise your free will think about the consequences.

When Sirach wrote about humanity he was really writing about how to treat your fellow person. He was providing advice and instruction on how one should conduct themselves among other human beings. This was probably the angel apparition speaking for him at the time. Many will argue in the modern world that he should be dismissed because he only addressed his writings toward men. However it must be understood that at the time he wrote it was man that had power and the ability to rule and create laws. Because of the culture of the time he might have realized that women would one day be given position of power but he also realized that his writings would be condemned if he proclaimed it.

The concept of purgatory achieved recognition somewhere around 1100 A.D. Many theological researchers claim that the concept of purgatory can be found in multiple passages of the new and the Old Testament. Its foundations come from the Jewish ceremony of cleansing after death. But in none of the teachings of Jesus is there a mention of purgatory. Now don't you think if a place like purgatory existed at least as described by the Catholic Church as temporary painful punishment to cleanse your soul before ascending into heaven that he would have mentioned it. Think about "oh by the way even if you do live a good life here on earth we're going to burn your soul for a while just so it'll be bright light by the time you come see me." Does that sound like it makes sense, because it does not. As I explained previously, free will gives you the choice to go from goodness to evil but nowhere in between. So if you live your life choosing sin or evil or anything that turns away from He who always was you can expect a one-way ticket to the other place. However if you try with all of your failings as a human being to keep the commandments and treat your fellow humans with respect then you have a one way ticket to heaven.

Is there any proof that this is true? The answer is yes and it is in the bible. When Christ was crucified between the good thief and the bad thief, Jesus proclaimed from the cross that the good thief would join Him that day in heaven. Whoops! What happened to the detour for cleansing? It was not acknowledged by Christ as He was dying so why is it so widely accepted now that Purgatory exists. This is the problem with most religions. They have embellished certain positions that increase their institutional influence on the individual instead of teaching the true word of He Who Always was. The word is kindness, something that most humans do not practice. Demons know that their responsibility is to promote hate and distrust. It is the only way that Satan can increase his ranks and his power. This is what feeds his ego and his own hatred of mankind. Most demons are followers and just want to be left alone which we are as long as we continue to promote the wishes of Satan and his inner circle. Unlike He Who Always was, Satan is not omnipotent. He cannot know everything. If he did, I would be shredded for dictating this autobiography and never be let loose again on earth. Most of what he learns is from other demons wishing favors or advancement in his ranks. We are a community of liars and backstabbers that have no feel for kindness toward our own kind let alone kindness to humans. Most demons actually hate their human hosts as I did in the beginning, but many learn that humans are just a tool to be used to accomplish further discord on earth and the continuance of our own existence outside the shredding.

Demons learned a long time ago that humans are motivated by greed and envy, This is the greatest weakness in humans. Churches actually promote these desires through their "do as I say not as I do" attitude. Even in times of great depression and human misery, religious institutions continue to bleed every last dime out of their congregations to improve their own position and domiciles. If only the church would listen to its own writings instead of banning the ones that made sense, they would realize that they would be stronger as a community than the general attitude of their congregations of being ignored today.

Again I have to refer to history to prove my case. The Catholic church proclaimed Thomas the apostle as a saint yet buried his writings in favor of Paul's. Paul never met Jesus, but Thomas spent most of his life with Him. When Thomas (the twin) wrote his own epistles, the church buried them and claimed that they were not authenticated. Few people realize that by referring to Thomas as the twin, it was a reference to the apostle's appearance and his resemblance to Jesus. Just as words are transcribed literally from language to language today, little consideration is given to inferences in the native language. Thomas was Jesus's twin in appearance. When Christ transcended and returned to earth Thomas of all disciples did not recognize him because Christ no longer looked like a twin of himself. The Gospel of Thomas was found among the Nag Hamadi scrolls and has been dated to 50 to 100 AD. Who better to offer insight into Christ than a person that was on the scene when Christ walked the earth, but instead the church gets its insight into Christ through an individual that never met Him and in fact persecuted his followers?

Thomas often portrays Christ's sayings as cryptic because Thomas was not very educated at the time he had been recruited as an apostle, but as his stewardship grew and his travels and preaching expanded to the east, he was obviously influenced by the current Indian culture of 50 AD. There again is historical proof that Thomas preached in India for many years and it can be concluded that he in turn was also influenced by the Buddhist culture of the congregation he formed. Throughout Afghanistan, Central Asia, and India, Buddhism dominated the population and there can be little doubt that some cross pollinations of beliefs occurred. So with the existence of first-hand knowledge of the beliefs of the center of the church, why did the Catholic church render Thomas's writings to obscurity?

Malfec looked up at Officer Rendell and said:

I'll have to put down the many thoughts of other demons on this subject at some other time in the future. I may have to write an entire book on the subject. There are many theories from the outcast because the decision to follow the writings of Paul actually helped cause world dissension whereas the writings of Thomas promoted inner and outer peace and introspection of all things. The ascetics of the world would have been better appreciated for their natural beauty if Thomas's writings were followed. Instead giant citadels, buildings and structures became the sought after beauty to seeking God by humankind. Stupid humans!

Rendell laughed. What makes you think you'll have time to write a book?

Malfec looked at her trying to assess if she was understanding what he was saying or was she humoring him to get a confession. What makes you think that my actions are so grievous that I'll even be prosecuted?

You killed three individuals and brutally mutilated their bodies.

I killed them because they were going to kill me and this host's brother.

So you cut off their arms and crushed their skulls?

That was to send a warning to their friends.

At this point the side door to the interrogation room opened and a grey haired man signaled for Officer Rendell to step out.

Before you go do you think I can get a drink of water?

The other officer spoke for the first time. You don't need a drink of water remember you are a demon.

He laughed as Rendell turned, scowled at the other officer and she said, "I'll get you a drink of water, be right back."

The other officer turned and looked at Malfec and said "Bullshit."

Chapter Twelve

America

Officer Rendell returned and handed Malfec a cup of water. Malfec stared at the water but did not drink it. He continued his story:

The Incan woke from his sleep and gazed at the destruction surrounding him. He thought the spirits of the forest had attacked the remains of the thieves. He was covered in blood and ran for a nearby spring. The cold water washed the dried blood off his body and he stuck his head under the water to get all the dried blood out of his hair. He was afraid and the cold water sent shivers through his body. He crawled over to the streams bank, stood up, and then he started running. I was not familiar with the stamina of Incan tribesmen but apparently they warm themselves by running and running for a long time. He was heading north and nothing was slowing his pace. He ran for the next three days covering almost 150 miles stopping only to eat fruit and sleep for short periods of time usually from midnight to first light of morning. On the fourth day he stopped running and only walked. As he walked he would stop and pick strange looking plants and chew on their roots. We walked for days and finally came upon an entire village of cliff dwellers. I thought that this might be the perfect opportunity for me to move on. I waited for a day and witnessed many introductions. Apparently this Incan was not a stranger to these people even though they were very different from him. For the first time in many centuries I ran into new foods and artifacts that I had never seen before. Every night the people of the village would climb up into the cliffs on ropes. As soon as everyone was in a shelter the ropes would be pulled into the caves and it became impossible to access the dwellings from the cliff floor. As the sun rose, the rays of the sun burst into the cave openings and the ropes dropped to the cliff floor. Men, women and children all exited at once from the wall of the cliff holes.

It was time I tried to jump into another being, so I picked a strong young brave and leapt from the Incan. I landed right on my ethereal ass on the desert floor. That was impossible. I jumped again into a young woman and once again I found myself on the ground. This was impossible. I did not need permission to temporarily take over a human. I leapt again toward an older female and found myself ricocheted across the canyon. This was very wrong and as I tried multiple leaps the local indigenous peoples began to seek out the nuisance that was pivoting through their numbers. Finally after becoming frustrated and a little angry I jumped back into the Incan. It was time to influence the host and get out of this village. We walked through the night as I tried to piece this puzzle together. I have never heard of a human that we could not leap into unless there was another fallen angel already within the human host. If these people were already possessed by my fallen angel brethren then I would have been immediately recognized for what I am, but there was no recognition. There was silence, blockage, rejection of my presence. I needed to converse with another fallen angel but out here in the middle of nowhere it would not happen. This was driving crazy. Part of me wanted to go back and try again but another part of me began to fear being trapped outside a host. If these people started to recognize me as an evil spirit they might have some preventative spells that might stop me from going back into the Incan. If that happened I could end up back in the nowhere and shredded. No way. Keep walking. Try to figure out what happened.

We were walking northeast and the weather started to turn colder. We eventually ran into a tribe of plains dwellers. They were migrating south east and without much effort I leapt into the first brave I saw. I travelled with this group for the next five years. I encountered my first view of the American Buffalo. This creature was majestic but to view a herd of a thousand of these creature thundering across the plains was magnificent. He Who Always was broke the mold when He created these creatures. There was a time when the tribe went on a hunt for meat. We crawled through the high plains grass and got within twenty yards of the great animal. When the signal was given we rose as one group and pursued the closest beast. The herd roared to life and human speech could not be heard above the hooves pounding the ground. As I rose to throw a spear, I heard a loud snort like a gun going off from my left. These people had no guns and the Spanish had not progressed this far north. It wasn't a gun, it was a large white buffalo that had been laying in the tall grass not ten feet away from me. When it rose to its full height it towered over the brave and was heading right for my host. It crashed into the brave with all of its power and I heard the bone break in his leg. He fell to the ground and a hoof hit him in the side of the head. The other hunters were scattering as the great white snorted loudly standing over the broken body of the brave. One hunter, who I believe was the brave's brother threw his spear at the buffalo but it bounced off his hide. The buffalo snorted again and reared on his feet, turned and galloped away. The other hunters rigged a gurney and they carried the body of the brave back to the encampment. When the body arrived, the storytelling began. At the same time the brave was carried to the medicine man's teepee. I could feel the brave's life beginning to ebb away. I looked squarely in the face of the medicine man and he knew what I was but he wasn't afraid. I leapt right into him. The brave died and stories of his encounter with the great white buffalo were told around the campfires for many moons. Meanwhile I enjoyed a peaceful existence as the medicine man of the tribe for the next ten years. I continued to leap into the descendants of the medicine man as the tribe continued to migrate further north toward what is known today as Canada.

Chapter Thirteen

Martyrs

By the time white men started to settle North America I had been with the tribes of the Iroquois nation for many years. I was established as a member of the Mohawks as a fairly well respected medicine man. I preached about the dangers of the white man and had aroused great suspicion with many of the members of the five tribes. The tribes allowed some of the settlers from the Dutch settlements to trade with the tribes for furs which were being shipped backed to Europe. I knew the ways of the Europeans but my last experience with them had been during the crusades and the papal conspiracies. Once again I began to notice the influence of the church on these new settlers and I cautioned the tribes about the deceit behind the false promises of the church. Many Indians do not believe in a soul transitioning to a better place when dead. They may believe in re-incarnation either in another human or an animal until the essence is purified and ready for finality or completion. The soul may make many journeys before it is done. When the soul has completed its final journey it is done. If you tell some Indian tribes that their soul will go on forever, you are telling them that they will never come to rest.

The Dutch traders were drunks and sought to mate with the Iroquois women. They would often invite the Mohawk and Iroquois braves into their camps where they would get them drunk then get them to bring their women into the settlement. There were no white women in the settlement and these traders had been without female companionship since they left Europe. The only reason the Indians did not kill the traders is because they wanted the whiskey they provided and they did not try to force their beliefs on them unlike the Jesuits that had made conversion inroads to tribes in the South. The word had travelled fast about the new religion being practiced by the southern tribes. The black robes were teaching about a savior, someone that would free the souls in the afterlife so that the soul did not have to jump from one creature to another in order to perfect itself. There was a rumor of a black robe that had escaped the Iroquois tribe known as the bear clan after he had been tortured and escaped back to Europe. Instead of staying there he returned to the same area and was trying to convert the very Indians that tortured him. The Iroquois admired this black robe named Isaac Joques and gave him the Indian name meaning the indomitable one. However, they also feared his teachings. The medicine men of the tribes were worried that the teachings of one God and one soul would weaken their authority. The black robes were teaching healing of the soul and were also able to heal the body with their medicine. There were those native peoples such as the Hurons that believed every word the black robes were preaching. They travelled with the black robes and were hated by the Iroquois. So when the indomitable one was recaptured by the Bear clan, there needed to be an example made to show the people that the black robes were not infallible. The bear clan asked me to travel to their camp to confront Isaac Joques and his party. He was brought to my tent and I could see that he immediately recognized me as one of the fallen angel. He said, "what are you doing among these people?"

I said, "I don't know what you are talking about."

Then in Latin he said, "Be gone unclean spirit."

I said in Latin, "Unclean, you have nerve, you are the one that wants to die for a belief that you cannot prove."

Then he said, "You have given me the proof that I need and I am ready to die in full confidence that today I will be with He Who Always was."

That's exactly what he said, but no one knew that is what we the outcasts call God. I watched as he got up and started to walk out of my tent. He was insulting a medicine man, but really he was insulting me, so I had no choice but to pick up a tomahawk and drive it into his neck. He fell out of my tent into the camp and died as the entire tribe witnessed his death. Some of the braves wanted to mutilate the body but I would not allow it, so they cut off his head and threw his body into the river. The rest of his party was killed the next day after the braves and warriors were up all night drinking whiskey and going crazy. I knew it was time to get out of here and get back to the world where I could roam freely from human to human.

Years later I would see a drawing on a map of the execution of the Jesuits and there in the middle of two priests was my image but it was the only face in the drawing that was distorted beyond recognition.

Chapter Fourteen

The French and Indian War

I continued travelling with the tribes and moved into the Canadian Wilderness as the British tried to colonize the new world. The French and British engaged in multiple battles and the French tried to drag the Indian nation into the battle at every turn. The winters were especially cruel to the tribes of the north and took its toll on the young, old and sick. The white man had brought illness to the tribes in the form of small pox and measles. The Indians had no immunity to these diseases and died in great numbers. Fort William Henry was the Indians revenge for the unwanted gifts of disease from the Europeans. The French had negotiated a surrender of the fort that allowed the British and their families to leave with all their wounded and their possessions. It had been a long campaign and the tribes that fought with the French had been promised the spoils of the fort once the British left. When the tribes saw that the soldiers were leaving with all their possessions the tribes thought they had been betrayed. There were many sick and dying within the tribal camps that could make good use of the blankets, food, livestock, and weapons that should have been left behind when the British left.

The word went out, mostly from myself and other medicine men, to kill the retreating British and take their possessions. By the time the warriors caught up with the retreating British troops the group with the possessions had already reached a protected settlement, so the warriors attacked the wounded, the women and the children. It was a massacre of gross proportions. Although I had not developed any feelings of pity for humans over the centuries, I soon realized that there was a savageness in the human spirit that I had never witnessed in the crusades or any time before. It was a beast that was growing in humankind and would later fester into massive world wars and beyond.

I had to leave this life experience as I could see the end of the Northeast Indian tribes was inevitable after the Fort William Henry massacre. I jumped into an escaping female who feared for her life and we made it to the settlement unharmed. Once in the settlement I found a young British Naval Officer that seemed to have some rank and lived in relative comfort for the times. He would be my ride for the next twenty years and this pairing would lead me right into the middle of the Revolutionary War. His name was Richard Howe.

Prior to my taking control of Howe, he had gained the reputation of a by-the-book officer of the crown. He was not known to take chances or to put his command in jeopardy. That would all change once I removed his fear of failure as I had no human inhibition. Live or Die, it did not matter to me. In the next sea battle of the Quiberon Bay, Howe was fearless. Of course he was because he was really me. His reputation carried back to England where he was rewarded with higher ranks and eventually became treasurer of the Navy.

Wealth was the power behind comfort and I realized that the best ways to accumulate wealth was to be near those with wealth and power. As Howe controlled a great fortune in the Navy's coffers that wasn't his to spend, the contractors that were the receptors of naval building contracts were themselves wealthy and were able to provide Howe access to opportunities not afforded the average English citizen. His wealth grew but when his old friend Ben Franklin let him or me, know that the colonies were going to secede from the crown he knew that he would be called back into action. He was appointed commander of the fleet in charge of the war in the Americas.

There were many times that I had to admire the seaworthiness of this man but I was not meant to spend my life at sea so as soon as the British hatched a plot to put a group of spies on shore in the colonies I jumped into one of these individuals and left the services of the British Navy. For many years afterward I followed the career of Admiral of the Fleet Howe and thought that I might have had some residual influence in his rise to acclaim. He was one of the few humans I had ever admired for his courage, conviction and honor.

Once I was ashore I had the British spy make his way to Concord and left his shell with British papers and currency to the local colonists to handle. In the meantime I had jumped into a scrawny old man way past the age of eligibility for recruitment by the colonist armies. He was a candle maker and happened to be the only candle maker in the town. I took a personal sabbatical from controversial matters while inhabiting this individual and relaxed for the next twenty years until the candle maker's heart started weakening. I happened to jump into the candle maker's neighbor in Concord and a strange twist of fate threw me right back into action. The house belonged to Jonathon Hildreth. Hildreth owned a saw mill in the north and lived at the house during the winter months when it was too hard to mill and transport lumber. The house was spacious and exuded wealth. Jonathan was on his third wife and she was far younger than he. His second wife had borne him several children who were now approaching adulthood. One of the young men was living with a young girl originally from New Jersey who doubled as a house servant. The father had a fight with the son over this living arrangement and asked the son to leave and take the whore with him. The whore was mindless at this point because I was now in charge. They both left but the son did not take the girl with him but instead abandoned her to the streets. Life for a single woman was unsettling in the religious oriented colonies of the north, so I decided to take the woman south toward the new Capitol. After all this was her original birthplace and therefore I was taking her home.

Her name was Lizzie Ann and when we arrived in the Washington area the country was changing. Washington had just gained self-governance from the Congress. Liz's father had been an overseer of one of the Maryland land owners and had been brutalized as a child. When she ran away she never thought she would ever come back to Washington but then again I was influencing her decisions. I knew we had to make some arrangements in order to settle down. There would be a lot of controversy that would be faced by a single woman living alone, so she had to find a man preferably one with some wealth. It wasn't difficult, all the farmers were in town to sell their crops and old man Jenkins was the perfect choice for this 26 year old female. Jenkins was 40 and lonely. His skin was weathered from years of toiling his father's farm of 900 acres. He was never married but he was getting on in years and very lonely. One look at Liz and he was smitten. He had her put up in a local boarding house and asked her to marry him after a short courtship. One year after marriage they had their first child a son and shortly after a daughter Mary. The children grew up wealthy land owners and each received extensive properties. When Liz developed an illness I jumped into the daughter Mary and stayed with her until her trial for complicity in the assassination of Abraham Lincoln. I should have stayed with her mother who lived another ten years but I had to jump while Mary was in prison as it became evident that she was doomed for the executioners gallows.

For the next thirty some years I never stayed in one host for more than two years. I believe my attitude toward humans was changing. I was no longer viewing them as objects to use but as vessels that were contributing to my own development. Although the only feelings that I possess is survival I sensed that with each jump I was becoming aware of a psychic link between the humans and myself. Perhaps this was because I could recall every moment I spent inside them and could replay those moments in slow motion remembering where I was and who I possessed. I didn't feel sorry for the things I had made them do or feel happy when I affected those around them but it was the memory in vivid details of these things that was changing the way I looked at them.

I tried to jump into a dog one time, but apparently only certain minor demons have that capability like the one that possessed Seraphim, Saladin's horse. When I tried to jump I thought I had been hit by a sledge hammer. I literally bounced off a brick wall near the trash cans the mutt was feasting near and went right back into the bum sleeping on the corner that I just left. Not to be defeated so easily, I tried again and the same thing happened. I tried a third and fourth time only sending the bum I kept returning to into a drunken stupor for my efforts. I needed to consult with other outcasts as I had stated I was a witness to the demon that took possession of Seraphim and I knew it could be done. This was akin to the forbidden fruit that Lucifer used to lure Adam and Eve from the Garden of Eden. The ability to jump into an animal could prove very beneficial to a member of the outcasts should they discover that their host was dying or trapped by those that can see us. An animal would be a perfect escape route.

In 1890 I happened upon a doctor in Syracuse, New York that was host to a high ranking member of the outcasts named Malik. Malik was so powerful that he had his own legion of outcast's servants that catered to his demands, which is rather unusual because we all have free will. That is why we were thrown out of paradise by Micha-el, because we exercised it. Malik was a specialist among demons and master manipulator. He had been on earth since the time of the Assyrians and was known to humans as a demon. Many stories had been written about him throughout history although few humans tied all the stories together as one entity. Without exception humans have referred to him through his known name without realizing that they were identifying the same entity. Although the outcasts know him as Malik, humans call him Moloch. He single handedly placed abortion in the forefront of the separation of the sexes empowering women to take back control of their lives from men or so they thought. His greatest accomplishment to date according to him was to have Ely van der Warkle publish an article on the practice and cost of abortion and then have van der Warkle address the Boston Obstetrical Society where he publicly stated "The luxury of an abortion is now within the reach of a serving girl." He went on to quote a price of $10 and state that it was available on installment plans. This was unbelievable in Lucifer's eyes and he made a deal with Moloch that he would increase his servant legions by one for every abortion that he or his following had performed. Unfortunately, you can't always trust Lucifer to keep the essence of a bargain and Moloch became the dumping ground for a lot of the lesser demons and bunglers that had been waiting millenniums to jump to earth. When they got here a lot did not know how to jump and ended up being shredded and recycled back several times. At one point Moloch said he actually had to hold a course on how to stay on earth.

Moloch confronted me at one point and said look Malfec, nothing is perfect he said, but some of these returnees were only good for dumping into the middle east and letting them rot in that desert environment where they could infest the growing unrest in that region and not be seen by the public for decades to come. I don't know what happened to these once angelic warriors that were now no smarter than dog meat. Their minds were shredded along with their bodies and they were a threat to us being discovered which would cause a renewal of religious fervor. Once they were let out of the nowhere and were able to jump into humans they were an embarrassment for the highest order. They turned into murderers, rapists, child pornographers and other openly lewd acts. Some came back four and five times and finally I had to stop what I was doing to get Lucifer's attention. He wanted to know why I froze my operation. I told him that I was a dumping ground for idiot outcasts and that I would not push his agenda until the agreement was re-written. Well you know his attitude toward renegotiating a deal. He blew his cork. I said I didn't care I wasn't doing a damned thing until the selection of candidates for my legion improved. He finally agreed if I would take one lesser demon for every three good ones. I agreed. So now I had to figure out what to do with the idiots I had and I remembered Seraphim. I told Moloch that I was there when that happened you know.

So Moloch continued, I contacted the demon that jumped into the horse to find out how he did it. He said that he had never jumped into a human, didn't like the looks of them and thought the horse was far more attractive. He looked into the eyes of the horse and wished to be one and BOOM, it happened.

So, I think I found the answer of what to do with all these losers that Lucifer was sending me. I took a couple of them to the local zoo first. I figured that if they jumped into animals that were locked up, no harm would come to humans and if it did they would blame it on the animal going wild. So I picked animals that were generally considered docile. First I tried the sheep, and the sheep were too stupid to be possessed. I already knew that a horse would be acceptable but really who would want a demon in a horse loose in civilization today. Maybe out west, but I didn't feel like travelling outside Syracuse. I tried a goat, and had a success of sorts. Once this idiot demon took possession the goat started ramming its head against a wall until it killed itself and out pops the idiot. I tried a salamander, realizing that Lucifer himself once took over a snake but never told the rest of us how he did it, again no luck, with the salamander. I tried a duck, a dove, a deer, and a wolverine and again no luck. We went through nearly every animal in the zoo with no success. Finally, I started thinking about the Seraphim incident and the experience with the goat. I realized that the idiot that jumped into the horse and the idiot that jumped into the goat had one thing in common, it was their first jump.

I shredded the idiot and grabbed another one from my legion and had it jump into a wolf. Success! The wolf was the perfect creature. They were mean, predatory, pack driven, and in this case confined because the entire wolf population of upper New York had been wiped out from the bounties placed on them. There were no ill effects and the wolf just went to sleep after devouring a pound of meat that was left in the cage. That was one down and about a thousand more to go before I could get rid of all the losers that I had received over the years. By the time the wolf died, they'd be shredded back in the nowhere and not my problem. I ran out of wolves of course but every new loser recruit I got I put into elephants, sharks, giraffes, zebras, and even tortoises.

Well, Malfec, when I found out I could pop these idiots into tortoises I just about had a heart attack I was laughing so hard. These creatures live for a hundred years and that's about how long it would take one of them to walk to New York city. I found the perfect vessel for idiots and I must have put some five hundred of them away. Anyway I kept trying different animals because there are only so many tortoises available. I tried cows which I thought would be a perfect place for these idiots because they were so plentiful. This seemed like a great idea until the cows got milked and the smell was so atrocious that the dairy farmers were killing the cows and inadvertently releasing the idiots inside back to the nowhere. Lucifer got wind of what I was doing when 20 of those losers got thrown back to the nowhere at once. The whole herd of cows was killed because the farmer couldn't sell the stinking milk. Now I am back on Lucifer's shit list but what do I care, all I have to do is increase the number of abortions out there and he'll be back to his dancing self.

Malik you have been promoting abortions for centuries but recently the publicity around this issue is growing. Your last host almost single handedly brought abortion in the United States to the front page of every newspaper in America. You jumped into the woman, Madame Restell and started advertising the practice all over New York. Hell, you ran up more advertising bills than Carter's liver pills. In the end before she could be tried in court and have public opinion turned against the practice you had her commit suicide. You are known as the murderer of children and are most hated by all the angels for possessing Herod at the time "you know who" was born. I came to you because I thought if anyone knew how to jump into animals it was you. I needed an escape route but you have enlightened me. I know that it would be impossible for me to jump into an animal after I have possessed so many humans. But I leave you with one question to mull over. How did Lucifer jump into a snake?

So my friend, that is not a riddle it is common sense. Lucifer had never jumped into anything before so it was his first time and probably his last. This was enjoyable but I have so much work to do. Malfec, there are great evil things expected of you. Don't disappoint us.

Chapter Fifteen

Evil Stinks

Have you ever smelled a dog's ear that is infected? Well that is what a truly evil human smells like to the outcasts. It is a sign to us outcasts that we do not need to possess that individual as they are already too far gone to exert the effort. The purpose of taking over a human was never to convert them to evil but as I stated previously, it was to give us a means of escaping the nowhere. Having fun with a human's subconscious is just an added perk that gives us a little pleasure. There are those outcasts like Malik, who have interpreted this opportunity as a mission. Other outcasts see it as a chance to win favor with Lucifer and his inner circle. What they hope to get out of that is beyond me. Lucifer has no more pull on earth then he did in heaven. I guess that is what most humans and angels do not understand. They are always looking for a purpose. They never stop to consider that the fact they are alive is purpose enough. Now of course the outcasts can stay on earth a lot longer than humans and in that respect humans view their few adult years on earth as something to be cherished. If they knew what awaited them on the other side of physical death, they would be constantly trying to find ways to die early. "He who always was" made it easy for humans. Just say you love him even though you never met him and you'll be rewarded with immortality, no physical stress, total knowledge, physical and mental perfection and never have a need for any possession. You don't need to eat, exercise, breathe, defecate, fornicate, bathe or work. Why would any human want to stay on earth if they knew what waited for them. The problem is that humans are basically egotistically stupid and as mentioned before they are getting dumber instead of smarter.

However there are those humans that walk the earth with nothing but disdain for other humans. There are many psychology reasons given by the so called liberal elite that try to excuse their behavior due to some impressionable event in their youth, but in reality they are just evil. The smarter evil humans cover up their intentions and thoughts with trappings of civility. They appear to other humans as cordial, pleasant, outgoing, friendly and good natured, but internally they are rotten to the core. Ted Bundy was an excellent example. Another outcast that actually had an encounter with Bundy described him as rotten meat covered in flies that had been left out in the hot sun too long. He was a walking bag of pus.

I often go walking on the streets of New York as there seems to be an over-abundance of evil in this city. The Outcasts generally prefer less squalid locations to inhabit but I like to venture into other realms of human nature from time to time. I walk down Broadway past Times Square and my nostrils almost immediately begin to flare. I may be walking by a cab and an aspiring actress with her manager may get out and I am overwhelmed by the stench they both put out. It hangs like a vapor in the air and one would think I had been tear gassed as they walk by. At times like this I often have to go running into side street alleys as my eyes start to glaze over from the stench. Sometimes I see a street person laying on a cardboard box and I have to lean over him just to get a scent of pure innocent air. This will usually clear the sinuses of my host who is also in respiratory distress from the transference of my persona onto my human ride. It seems that after a prolonged time residing in a host, an outcast can have direct influence on the human host's sense of smell. I don't know why this is, but I began to notice it around the turn of the twentieth century. I was in Baltimore Maryland in the downtown district near the inner harbor. There were plenty of humans milling about shops and street vendors were selling their goods. The human I inhabited at the time was a professional baseball player named Frank "the Monkey" Foreman. He was on the Oriole's team as a relief pitcher at the time but I jumped in around the time he was pitching for the Cincinnati Reds.

By the way, baseball is the only real sport in the eyes of the outcasts. No matter where they are in the world, if you really want to get into a good argument with one of your own, mention your favorite team and wham, bam, what the hell, you are in a brawl, especially if the other outcast is a

Boston fan. Now you see the outcasts have an advantage because we can recall all the statistics from every player and every game that ever took place in any league. Yes, we are that anal. The other important thing to know about the outcasts is that they can actually impart the knowledge to their hosts as long as they are present in them. Don't ask me why baseball has emerged as a passion among us temporary earth dwellers, it must have something to do with our past. Baseball is pure. It isn't about hurting the other players, it isn't about individuality, it isn't about one player turning the tide of the game or dominating your opponent, it is about coming together in time as one group to collectively demonstrate mastery over a ball, a bat, and a glove and then try to do it again and again and again. How cool is that. If I ever had a say in heaven before I was kicked out I would recommend that everyone play baseball. Unfortunately that will never happen. So, we enjoy it here on earth through the modern centuries and hope that the sport is never usurped by the stupidity of soccer and basketball. These are two games truly inhabited by morons and the DUH Group.

Going back to Baltimore inner harbor, I was strolling down Light Street toward Battery Square and a young boy shouted out my name and asked for an autograph. I always liked to please my fans even though I wasn't the lead pitcher on the roster at the time. I was soon surrounded by young boys asking me to sign anything that they had that I could write on, when all of a sudden my eyes watered and my nostrils ingested the foulest smelling odor I had ever encountered. At first I tried to look around to see if someone had thrown out a bunch of dead crabs, but the streets were clean. The only smell I was used to down by the water was old man Willoughby McCormick's spice store and the Domino Sugar refinery. I looked up and saw a man about six foot tall punching the boy whose baseball I had just signed. I had to restrain my demon nature which was rapidly rising to the point it had risen when I inhabited the young Inca warrior many centuries ago. I don't know what was causing this internal reaction to seeing a human even though a youth, being flailed by this obviously obese and cruel man. I pulled back my pitching arm and let it fly without much regard for "the monkey's" pitching career. I felt the cartilage in the man's nose shatter and exude from his nostrils at the same time I heard the thunderous crack. The big man fell to the brick street and banged his head and was immediately knocked unconscious. My first reaction was to pounce on the downed human and take his life away, but I heard the sound of clapping in my head as all the young boys and other people in the crowd that had gathered start cheering for me. They were cheering for one of the outcasts and they didn't even know it. The crowd whisked me away to a local tavern when they heard the whistles of the police coming from the north on Light Street. While I had to let Frank take the credit for my act of ferocity, I never forgot the smell that surrounded that individual nor did I ever forget the reaction of the crowd. It made me realize that humans are basically frail and that they recognize evil but they are often powerless to confront it because of laws put in place by other evil humans to protect themselves from having decent humans turn on them. These evil humans are basically cowards and the only way for humans to overcome these evil cowards is for decent humans to emerge as leaders. Stand up for those that are helpless and weak. Lead people away from bullies and corrupt politicians assuming leadership roles at all costs by confronting them. And so that is why I troll the streets of New York, one of the most corrupt cities on the planet.

Whenever I am in New York today my favorite place to sniff out corruption is Manhattan. However, in the early nineteen hundreds it was the five points where evil festered. I have to admit that at this point I became an evil junkie. I really wanted to pound the shit out of bad guys. The population of five points around Mulberry had quadrupled in less than ten years from all the immigrants coming into New York. The corruption was rampant with the powerful taking advantage of the weak. It is one thing to offer services and make a profit from your clients; it is another thing to rob your clients of everything they have under false pretenses and empty promises. So, Five Points became my hunting ground for human miscreants and I must say there was no shortage of prey. I jumped from one human to another that I could tolerate due their minor corruption schemes but the really evil humans I needed to eliminate. There were many murders from 1903 to 1915 in and around New York that I had orchestrated but I also found out that other outcasts had also grown distaste for the filth that was walking New York streets. They also participated at times or acted as witnesses for the human I was using. The first group that was targeted was associates and members of the Morello gang. The Morello's were a powerful family that ran most of southern Manhattan. They were violent and criminally artistic in the execution of their perceived enemies. The famous case of the death of Benedetto Madonnia had all the trappings of a Morello execution. Madonnia's body was found cut up and placed in a barrel and thus the legend of the barrel murders of New York was pasted across the New York papers. Madonnia, was of course just one of the executions performed by the outcasts over the next fifteen years. Evidence left at the scene often pointed to other gang members that were considered less corrupt then the ones being targeted. One such individual was Aniello Prisco. Zopo as he was known, was a two bit street hustler until the demon known as Mordac took him over. Mordac had been on earth longer than I had but received his name on his first jump from the nowhere. He jumped into Mordac the Viking from Verdun and the name stuck through the ages. Mordac was also short for biting or sarcastic, but Mordac took it literally. Every victim of Mordac had bite marks somewhere on their body. Over the next six years, Zopo the Gimp with direction from Mordac had been arrested for murder five times and each time there was not enough evidence. Either witnesses failed to show up, thanks to me, or no one saw anything and could not identify who pulled the trigger again thanks to several outcasts all jumping into witnesses at the right time. Finally, Mordac complained that he was losing control of the human and the stink was driving him crazy so he asked that we execute Prisco and send him back to the nowhere where he could be shredded and reconstituted. I jumped into a punk named Johnny Russo and had him pump two bullets into the back of the head of Zopo the Gimp. Russo was arrested but released when he claimed self-defense. Even the police were corrupt.

And so it went in our orchestrated elimination of gangsters and paid off politicians until World War I broke out and it was party time again.

World War I was the largest gathering of the outcasts that ever gathered on earth. There were many renewed encounters throughout Europe as the war escalated. There were no restrictions practiced by either side when it came to mass killing. There seemed to be a thrill tempting fate knowing the possible outcome of a jump may send you back to the nowhere and shredding. However, Lucifer was popping so many of the outcasts out of the nowhere we were betting on it being a short stay.

The allies were the first to unleash massive mortar bombardments on dug in troops on the German side and the Germans retaliated with huge clouds of mustard gas. A gas attack gave us some time to jump since death was not as immediate as a mortar round. The gas attacks seemed to occur in pockets and usually on a day when the wind wasn't blowing, so we forced our hosts to be more daring on those days than on days when steel was raining down from the sky. Fellow demons were flying back and forth across the battlefield, switching sides as the tide would change from one side to the other. British, French, German, and Russian hosts were falling like crazy. This was a blood fest to beat all blood fests for the outcasts. There were volleys of fires where hosts would be ripped to shreds and those outcasts that were too slow to jump were shredded and sent to the nowhere. I had jumped into one Brit foot soldier on the first day of the battle of the Sommes. He was scared to death of dying. He was buried so deep in a mud hole that other soldiers were stepping on his body without even knowing that he was in there. All of a sudden I heard someone yelling at the top their lungs that Lieutenant Harry was missing. Where the bloody hell Is Harry a captain yelled. I was a little dazed and was trying to figure out who the hell Harry was since I had just jumped from the German side. The soldier I was now inhabiting was so covered in mud that I didn't know what rank or whose side he was on. I carefully got up, brushed some of the mud away and sought to jump out of trench and get back into the fight. The soldier's name was Robert Quigg and as I jumped out of the trench toward the German front, I heard a voice screaming for help from my right. It was in my nature to ignore the wounded as they just got in the way of the fight, but this Robert Quigg shocked the hell out of me as he gained control of his own body and ran to the screaming wounded soldier. He picked up the soldier and ran back to the trench. He was helped into the trench with the dying soldier and then I got up and climbed back over the trench toward the front. This time I had picked up a rifle with a bayonet. I was hot for blood. Then again I heard another scream and again Robert Quigg ran to the wounded soldier and this time threw him over his shoulder and carried him back to the trench dropping the rifle in the process. This was the first day of the Battle and it was gearing up to be one bloody mess. Back in the trench, someone gave Robert a drink of water and up we went again. This time I found a revolver that I was going to fire it one way or another. We didn't get thirty feet when a bloody hand in a mud bog sticking up started shaking. The hell with that I thought but Robert dove into the bog pulled the soldier out with a sucking sound as the water and mud slid from the soldier's body. This time the wounded soldier was so soaked that it was impossible to lift him. Robert dragged him inch by inch back to the trench. This was getting ridiculous, I was losing time, so I got Robert over the lip of the trench and started crawling to the front line. I still had the revolver and was digging under some barbed wire and my hand touched a body. It was still warm but obviously so badly wounded that he was not going to make it. Out pops Robert. He grabs the bloody body and pulls it out of the mud under the barbed wire. Roberts arm got caught in the wire and his blood started to pour out of the cut. He grabbed the shoulders of the wounded man and started crab walking backward. A machine gun opened up from somewhere to the right and the front. I felt the whiz of the bullets and I think one creased his back. Pulling the wounded man inch by inch he managed to get the soldier back to the trench. We quickly passed the wounded soldier over to a medic and this time a Sargent grabbed my arm and said that's enough son. I looked at him with fire in my eyes and said so why aren't you out there. With that I leapt over the lip of the trench and slogged as fast as I could toward the front. There were shots being fired all around me because this time I was standing straight up running like a banshee. That's because I found out that this was an Irish Rifle Battalion that Robert and his buddies in the trench were assigned. Banshees, Irish anybody get it? Oh well, I found myself singing "to the front, to the front, to the front, front, front." All of a sudden a mortar went off not ten feet away and I fell ass over elbows right onto a pit of bodies. Just my luck, Robert jumps into action again and I can't stop him. He starts feeling for pulses and comes across a body that looks dead to me but he grabs the body and whispers into the ear of the soldier, don't worry buddy I got you. He lifts the guy on our back and starts running back as fast I was running to the front. We heard the machine gun rip up the ground behind us as Robert leaps into the air over the trenched edge. I thought we were going to have a hard landing but instead five Irish riflemen caught us in the air. Wounded soldier and Quigg, we never touched the ground. I yelled thanks, rolled over on my side and up I went determined to get into the action before the day was over. I managed to get Robert all the way to the German forward trench, a position that a small British advance unit had breached earlier that morning. Now it was heavily fortified with machine guns and sniper fire. New barbed wire had been strung across the German trench where they were dug in for the night. This had been a long day and I was sneaking up to their defenses. I was within five feet of the lip of their trench and ready to pop in the face the first German I saw. Damn if a German didn't leap over the wire and landed right on top of me. I was ready to deliver a deadly blow with a pipe I had found in the mud when I recognized Jasper a fellow outcast. He said, "Malfec, holy shit what are you doing here?" The same thing you are. "SSSHHHH" they might here us he said. So this is awkward. Do I kill you or should you kill me?. No. I said. I haven't been able to kill anybody all day, this host I am in keeps dragging wounded people back to the British trench. "Well I can kill him after you jump into one of the Germans if you like" Nah, I said, I am still trying to get control of him, Every time he sees a wounded buddy, I lose control. How about your host. I could kill him and you could jump back into the German line. "Malfec, you are a real character. I'm kind of a hero on the German side and this is really great for my ego." Shit Jasper, I have to get this guy to kill somebody if he is ever going to be a hero. "You know Malfec, there are some really trashed Austrian troops to the south that might be easy kills for your host and his friends" Well Jasper, I'll pass that along when I get back, in the meantime don't forget to jump before your host dies or its back to the nowhere. "Ah Shit! At least I'll have plenty of company." We both laughed, and then a cry of pain came from somewhere to the left. It was a Brit crying and I knew the Germans were probably targeting the wounded Brit so they could snipe anyone that tried to rescue him. Up jumps Robert Quigg and runs for the soldier. The Germans in the trench were so surprised to see the enemy that close, they just stood there and watched as Robert Quigg ran over fifty yards without being shot. All of a sudden Jasper's host stands up straight and starts clapping for Robert Quigg. The Germans in the trench also start clapping and cheering as Robert darts for the wounded soldier. Suddenly a sniper's shot rang out as Robert Quigg dives for the foxhole where the cries were coming from. Once again, He throws the wounded soldier over his shoulder and starts to crawl with the man on his back. Again the Germans start to clap and cheer. No shots are being fired.

Robert stands up straight as the Germans clap louder and louder. Then all of a sudden from the British trenches clapping and cheering also started up. For the entire length of the front between the two lines no shots are being fired as Robert walks to the British trench. He is welcomed with open arms and louder cheers ring out from both sides. Robert Quigg became the hero of the Battle of the Sommes and never fired a single shot that day.

War Council of Demons

There were so many outcast angels on the battlefield, someone decided that a war council be convened so that some rules could be established to indicate those hosts possessed on both sides. The reason for this was predicated on one of Lucifer's favorites getting sniped by another outcast without realizing he had just sent back a favored outcast to be shredded. In fact, this was happening so often that we needed a way to identify who was fighting. A simple solution was needed but it couldn't be so obvious that any human would soon discover that those with the sign were not being killed or even wounded. A plan had to be hatched that worked for both sides but that would keep the bloodshed flowing. We knew that there would still be accidents but at least we could reduce the numbers shredded. It was decided that the worst case was when one soldier would sneak up on another that was a host but if killed would immediately be sent back to the nowhere. So the sign decided upon would be simple but obvious but apply to both sides.

It was decided that the trigger finger on the right hand extended forward on the trigger guard would be the perfect signal that would give the aggressor a signal to make sure the intended target was not one of the outcasts. As long as everyone remembered to do this it worked well but there were some that would get so involved in their blood rapture that they forgot and were targeted by other outcast angels. Others that were shredded happened to have jumped into a host that was left handed. I personally took out one of the outcasts who recognized me as he was ripped from the host and I heard him yell "Malfec, you asshole." At any rate Lucifer was happy with the arrangements we had made at the war council which spread rapidly among the all the fallen angels. For the next two years it appeared that this blood fest would never end. Then, as suddenly as the war started, the war ended. There were minor outbreaks that continued to flare up but nothing of note.

I was jerked back to the present as the tall police officer slaps me in the head.

Officer Rendell is getting tired of my story and wants to address the reason I am sitting in this room in handcuffs. I asked a simple question, where is my brother? I am told he was safe and sitting in one of the witness rooms. I explained that he has downs syndrome and you would have thought I was speaking a foreign language. Don't they teach cops anything? Probably not, most of them only have a high school education. Many of them were jocks, C students, lacking any worldly experience. Some may have a military background but not usually the female officers they are part of the upward mobility push for equal opportunity. I started to speak and continue my story when all of a sudden I was hit in the back of the head again by the male officer, which had moved out of my line of vision. My head snapped forward and I heard him say "Shut up." I said what the hell is wrong with you? He said shut up and hit me again in the head. My head snapped forward against the table. I said, "I want to see my brother." He said "tell us what happened, enough of this other shit. Are you trying to appear insane?"

I said, "I am telling you the truth and you know it."

Then Officer Rendell said, "Let him talk, eventually we will get to the twentieth century and maybe then he will fill us in on the truth."

"If you let me finish I'll tell you exactly what happened, are we still being taped?" Rendell said, "Why? Are you hoping we will run out of video tape? Well that won't happen, but hurry it up, I have to get home to my kids."

If you let me finish I will get to the truth.

After World War I there was jubilation around the world. Soldiers were returning home. There had never been so many soldiers with injuries that would stop them from returning to productive lives. Many of them turned to alcohol to heal their wounds. This was especially the case in the mining regions where a large majority of American soldiers had returned home only to find the mines closed or abandoned. Alcohol was the favorite past time and when it became so wide spread many of the genteel society started to object to open drunkenness. Prohibition caught on and Congress signed into law the eighteenth amendment. So, alcohol went underground. The United States was not prospering and in many of the major cities crime was rampant. In the outskirts of the cities rum running was a popular way to earn extra money. I will save describing my experience during that era for another time.

There were many rumors that there was trouble brewing in Europe and that Germany was once again becoming very powerful.

The tall Officer spoke up, "We know that shit head. We all studied history."

"You can read?"

Again, he hit me in the back of the head. I was getting tired of this and felt that I wasn't going to be able to go on with this goon in the room. However, I needed this story on tape. Apparently, whoever was watching from the other side of the glass saw what was happening and opened the door and told the other cop to leave. He did but came right back in.

"Thought you got rid of me didn't you?"

I said "Your time will come."

World War II

When WWII broke out I was being hosted by a Naval Officer named Ralph. He was an Ensign and stationed on an LST that was only in port for minor repairs. After a night of celebrating in the local bars he returned to West Loch marina of Pearl Harbor just in time for morning muster. Other crew members were also returning to the ship that had permanent residence near the base with their families. The sirens started about 7:48 in the morning as the duty section was being inspected in dress white uniforms. Battle stations! Battle Stations! This is not a drill, Rang out over the 1MC as the claxons from all the ships in the nest went off. Gun turrets were being manned and everyone was looking to the skies as squadrons of aircraft flew over the harbor. The explosions were heard first and then felt but no attention was being paid to the LSTs.

Black smoke was seen rising from the main harbor. More explosions and then return gunfire was heard. The word was being spread that we were under attack but there was no indication that this was occurring at our location. After several hours the attack ceased but the fires continued. It appears that I had missed the action but this was just the start of a conflict that would last many years and I would ride this host all the way to Mindoro Bay in the Philippines.

Listen butthead said the tall officer, if you think we are going to sit here and listen to your happy killing adventures in the Pacific you can suck an egg. I want to know why you killed those three men. You obviously had an advantage and lured them into an ambush. You viciously mutilated them and made sure they were dead.

Malfec: Hey, if you don't want to know, that's cool I'll just shut up and you can figure it out yourself.

Officer Rendell: That's enough, Please go on, but can you save the WWII adventure for another time.

Malfec: Sure I'll skip it and come forward to the present. Where's my brother?
He's a Cherub.

At one time I looked up the word Cherub. According to Wikipedia Cherub is short for the Hebrew Cherubim, but what I didn't know was that the entity called a Cherub was known to the Assyrians, Akkadians, Babylonians and the Mesopotamians. It was said that the Akkadians believed that Cherub meant blessed. In truth, the cherubim angels were the companions of He Who Always was. Their duty was to always be by his side. That was there only duty. When the son came to earth in human form many legions of Cherubim were assigned to accompany him on earth, which is what they did until he turned thirty years of age. They were all dismissed by the Son as He set out to complete the great plan which to this day the outcasts have no knowledge. Unfortunately the Cherubim assigned to Him were left on earth. They like the outcasts soon learned to take hosts but they unlike the outcasts were pure angels and could not jump into any human. So they learned that they could jump into unborn children of holy women. They did this reluctantly at first but later they were prolific when they became lonely. There was a down side to these beings taking over an unborn. All the possessed children developed downs syndrome. These are the purist of human beings. They do not hate. They do not sin. They require little or nothing from this world. They are happy to love just as their angel possessors love He Who Always was. Their purity comes from deep inside their being and their mind. Even the outcasts respect their presence and still consider them our brothers. It just so happens that the human I possess has a Cherubim for a brother and I would allow myself to be shredded before I let any human harm him.

Malfec in a Loud eerie voice screamed: Let Me See HIM.

The glass in the viewing window shattered and the walls began to shake.

Officer Rendell: What the hell is going on?
Other Officer: It's an earthquake, it will pass.
Officer Rendell: Did he cause it?
Other Officer: Don't be absurd. Are you starting to believe this bullshit?
Malfec: You know it is me, now show me my brother.

Again the building shook and rumbling noises and alarms started sounding. Then suddenly, everything stopped.

Officer Rendell: Let him see his brother.
Other Officer: Are you crazy? Why?
Officer Rendell: Because that innocent person in the other interview room is starting to get scared and keeps asking for this piece of shit.
Other Officer: What is he calling him, because we still have no first name.
Officer Rendell: He calls him Beel.
Other Officer: You mean Bill?
Officer Rendell: Maybe that's it, probably but he doesn't say it that way. He has no identification on him either. So the only thing we have to go on is an old rental car agreement we found in the truck used at the crime scene. It is registered to a Tom W. Brant.
Other Officer: Hey Tom!

There is no reaction from Malfec. Both officers shrug their shoulders at the same time.

A third officer brings the man with downs syndrome into the room and he runs to Malfec's side and asks why his brother is handcuffed. Officer Rendell puts her hand on his shoulder and says it's alright it is just to keep him safe. The brother smiles and says OK, "can I have a coke? The third officer says sure you can and leads him out of the room toward the coke machine. As they walk down the hallway, Malfec hears the officer say "I have a brother just like you and I know he would be happy to meet you" then he hears his angelic brother say "Yes I know him, his name is San-De. "The officer was heard saying, that's his nickname how did you know that? But what the officer heard was Sandy not the angelic name of "San-De." Then he heard his human brother say "I don't know?"

Malfec: Are we ready to continue?

Rendell looking frustrated said, "No, put him in a cell and start cleaning up this mess. Then I am going home for the night."

Rendell went home and the night shift came on. When dinner was served one of the guards with oriental features dropped the tray as he approached Malfec's cell.

Tôi biết bạn quỷ he screamed. He was Vietnamese. I knew the words, he recognized me for my true self. He said, "I know you, Demon." How he knew what I was not sure. Was it me that he recognized or another outcast. I was in Vietnam and I took part in many operations that destroyed whole villages but I did not recognize this individual. The first thing I thought of was My Lai. Son My village March of 1968. My host had enlisted in the Navy and was quickly trained in jungle warfare. He was assigned to special operations with an Army detachment that was supposed to be providing him an escort to Dak To in order to meet up with other special forces. Charlie Company was a group of combat weary soldiers that had seen too much death. One of their fellow soldiers had wandered off the trail on an overnight patrol and they found him tied to a tree with his genitals hanging around his neck and his intestines lying on the ground. He was still alive, at least for a short while after they found him. Another of their company had stepped on some Punji sticks dipped in excrement. They had to amputate his foot. Two other members had been shot by a sniper on a patrol through what was supposed to be a friendly village. These guys were wired tight. There orders were to take me through the jungle to Dak To which meant we had to pass through Son My village. Their platoon leader was a green second lieutenant that lacked combat experience but had a preconceived notion that all Gooks were the enemy. He was on edge all the time. As we approached the village some of the villagers had gathered outside a hooch. They were nervous and kept looking inside the hooch. One of the ARVN soldiers told them to move away from the doorway. He started screaming at them and one of them an old woman ran inside the hooch. One of the members of the 1st platoon sprayed the grass hut and kept firing. All hell broke loose and all the soldiers kept firing including the 2nd Lieutenant. He said keep firing. I ran around the back of grass hut and saw a family escaping up a trench. I took out the two men with the group and saw a young boy turn to look at me. That's when I remembered. He yelled, "Tôi biết bạn quỷ". I had no idea what the hell he was saying and didn't. I did ask a translator later and learned that the young boy was yelling "I know you, Demon." He could see my true form. So here he was in this jail years later and he was my jailer. I better not sleep this night. When the trials started on the My Lai massacre, I was not included as my real mission was still classified and could not be released to the public. I did make my way to Dak To but not with Charlie Company. I met up with some Recon Rangers and we traversed the enemy lines to meet up with the unit I was assigned to lead and work our way north. A year after the My Lai massacre, the Army was called to task and court martial proceedings hit the news media back in the US. In his defense, Calley was screwed. He was given up to appease the American liberal public. What civilians fail to realize is that people die in wars. You can't have a war without people dying, especially when the enemy inter-mingles with the local population and coerces them to support their cause. This type of enemy is a coward. They want innocent civilians to die because they are so miserable that seeing innocent civilians mutilated and killed by real soldiers bolsters these coward's egos. I often felt that if civilians were not so passive, they would turn on these cowards and not provide them any kind of support but would point them out for the cowards that they are and allow real soldiers to take them out. However this scenario still plays out even today with the cowards of Hamas in Palestine. They are pigs and they deserve to die like the cowards they are for hiding in hospitals and schools. If the Palestinian people would give their names and locations to Israel or even uncorrupted Palestinian police they would not have the courage to continue to hide rockets in schools. These are shameful cowardly individuals that hide behind innocent civilians in the name of their prophet causing religious and pious people to fear violating their beliefs and therefore the innocent keep quiet while they are being persecuted and used as human shields.

Yes I am a Demon, but I do not fear cowards such as Hamas, Viet Cong, AL Qaida, and ISIS. I and all my fellow outcasts have a basic disdain for these groups and believe me, when they get to the nowhere they won't be meeting virgins and they'll be wishing that they didn't have sexual organs. They will never see paradise, they will never live in peace, they will never see each other. They will become the play toys for some of the most perverted outcasts in the nowhere.

There are no outcasts in the ranks of these terrorist groups, as they are already tainted and as I stated before they stink.

Chapter Sixteen

The long night.

I do not need sleep but the host I inhabit does. This night I needed to keep him awake. I did not feel comfortable with the guard recognizing my true nature. He had a gun and if I slept then he could end this host's life and I'd end up in the nowhere shredded again and waiting to come back. I had already spilled my guts on tape and if the tapes would be released prematurely, Lucifer would find out and I'd be the one regretting eternal life in the nowhere. I had to stay awake until Officer Rendell returned and restarted the interview. Around 3 am I heard some shuffling coming down toward the cell I was in. It was the officer that could see that I was an outcast and he looked very strange. He carried something in his hand but I couldn't make it out. It looked small and square.

As he got closer I could see the look on his face and the sharp look in his eyes. He walked with confidence and fear at the same time. He raised the object he held and I backed into the cell in case he decided to shoot me, I yelled wait, I have to tell you something. He looked at me and said you will die tonight. He raised the object and as he did a glimmer of light hit it and I saw that it was a book. The title was the "Rite of Exorcism." He really did know who I was. This could not be happening. This was not the plan. I approached the cell door and I said wait, I have to tell you something.

Officer: "I will not listen to your lies, you lying demon."

Malfec: "No, No, Listen."

Officer: "I will not listen to you."

Malfec: "You must, this body I am in is dying." "This man has cancer and will die soon, but he must stay alive long enough to save his brother." "Then if you wish you can exorcise me, cause I cannot leave here." "I will not leave here." "Do you understand what I am saying."

Officer: "Lies and more lies."

Malfec: "Is my brother in the room next door?"

Officer: "You have no brother, demon." "That poor man next door is mentally disabled." "Did you do that to him?"

Malfec: "No, He is this man's real brother and I am trying to save him."

Officer: "Enough lies, In the name of the Father, the Son..."

Malfec: "Stop! Please stop."

Officer: "That's what I said when you shot my father and brother. Do you remember, Demon? I looked right in your eyes and those same words and you shot again and again."

Malfec: "Yes I remember but I didn't shoot you, your sister, or your mother." "You lived and you are here to day."

Officer: "And Now I will send you back to hell."

Malfec: "Listen to what I am going to say, you know who I am and you know what I can do. If you continue with your idea I will find every sin and contemptible thing you ever did, send that out to all my demon bothers and they will come after your soul and your family. You should be very afraid of me because you know what I am and I will do what I say."

Officer: "You are foul and I don't believe you, you lie."

Malfec: You know I wouldn't lie about this, now turn around and leave, go home, and I will forget this ever happened."

As my face started to glow in the dark, which was a trick I had picked up from a magician I once rode, I could see the officer getting scared. He backed up and I let out a roar and fortunate for me the building started to rumble probably from one of the aftershocks of the earthquake we had earlier.

He dropped the book and ran. I was never so relieved. I knew I could let my host sleep and get ready or the next day. I really didn't have the power to do what I said but it seemed appropriate to try anyway. I didn't even know if he still had a family and most outcasts believe that if you get into a mess you are on your own. It was time to sleep.

Chapter Seventeen

Precinct Day 2

The rest of the night was uneventful as nights in prison go. There were men screaming in their sleep and I heard grunting from a cell down the hall. Since I was charged with murder I guess they didn't want to put anyone else in my cell just in case. I was escorted to the interrogation room and the one officer from yesterday was present but not Officer Rendell.

Malfec: Where's Officer Rendell.

Other Officer: She is running late she had a doctor's appointment not that it's any of your business asshole.

Malfec: Are we being recorded?

Other Officer: Yes.

Malfec: What is your name, you haven't told me your name?

Other Officer: Are you stupid, can't you read? What does the nametag read?

Malfec: So you want me to call you Morris?

Other Officer: That's Officer Morris to you.

Malfec: Yeah! Right.

Officer Morris: Start talking about what happened in the parking lot.

Malfec: I think I'll wait for Officer Rendell.

Officer Morris: Suit yourself I really don't give a shit however long this takes.

Malfec: Let me see my brother?

Officer Morris: Social workers took him away this morning.

Malfec: You'll regret that you pig. You should have let me see him. You know how important it was that he felt safe before he was turned over to strangers. You have no remorse. Well, tell them they can stop recording I won't be talking until I see Officer Rendell.

Officer Morris: Do you want a lawyer?

Malfec: No you asshole I want Rendell.

Officer Morris: Take him back to the cage.

A uniformed officer enters the room. He is real young and looks embarrassed. Hey, Morris there's a mob outside the precinct and a bunch of local TV stations.

Officer Morris: What are they saying.

Uniform: I don't know but they are carrying signs that say "We want justice" and "Another black crime unsolved"

Morris: Are they all Black?

Uniform: Pretty much except for the TV crews.

Morris: How many ?

Uniform: About a hundred but more keep appearing.

Malfec: Well. Well, guilty before charged. The poor black criminals were beaten and killed and a seventy year old whitey done it.

Morris: Shut up. We are way past lynch mobs.

Malfec: Want to bet?

Uniform: Morris, they are coming up the steps.

Morris: Tell the Desk Sergeant to send some uniforms out there and break them up.

Uniform: OK but I don't know if that will do any good with the TV crews there.

Outside on the street: "This is Nancy Gates with Channel 3 News downtown at the 69th precinct where an unknown white male is being held for the killing and mutilation of three black youths. Preliminary reports from the scene of the crime indicate that the three men had crushed skulls and multiple broken bones. One youth was said to have a tire iron sticking out of his eye. There has been no information provided by the police as to the identity of the individual that committed this crime, but it has been reported that another man in the car of the perpetrator was released to social workers and is not being interrogated by the police. It is believed that the individual turned over to social workers is mentally impaired and merely stayed in the vehicle the entire time the three males were tortured and killed. The identity of the mentally impaired man was only known as Sandy. This is Nancy Gates reporting. As we learn more we will keep you informed. I'll now turn you over to Tom Kinnan who has been interviewing members of the crowd gathering in front of the precinct.

Cameraman: Nancy, what the hell are you trying to do, cause a race war. You know that those so called three black youths were members of a street gang. They have rap sheets as long as my arm. They were probably trying to rob the poor bastard in the jail. Just because you're black, you always want to incite trouble every time there is a white on black issue.

Nancy: That's bullshit! Those young men were brutally killed.

Cameraman: Yeah and they probably deserved what they got. Would you even be reporting this, if the two white guys had been found dead and robbed in their car?

Nancy: No, that wouldn't be a story.

Cameraman: screw you.

Back in the Precinct Officer Rendell returns. Sorry I'm late. The doctor's appointment took longer than I anticipated.

Desk Sergeant: Is everything alright?

Officer Rendell: I don't want to discuss it. Where's the suspect.

Desk Sergeant: He's back in the cage, he wouldn't talk to Morris. He wanted you.

Can you have him brought to the room? Thanks.

In the room Malfec sees Rendell and smiles. It is good to see you again Officer Rendell. I really like the smell of you perfume.

Officer Rendell is caught off guard. Don't bullshit me; I'm not in the mood.

Malfec looks down at his manacled wrists. I understand my apologies.

Officer Rendell: What do you mean you understand, you have no idea about anything?

Malfec: I know your Doctor's visit didn't go well.

Officer Rendell: How do you know that?

Malfec: Have you not been listening to anything I have been saying? That's right you're still a skeptic. Well the doctor has given you six months before your condition degrades to the point you'll have to quit work, and then you have maybe another three months before they have to hospitalize you and then, well you know the rest.

Officer Rendell: What? I haven't told anyone, how do you know?

Malfec: Because I am what I told you I am. This body I am in is also dying but I can't help it because of its age. I have been here too long and now it is time for me to move on.

Officer Rendell: You're not going anywhere; in fact you might be spending the rest of your life in jail.

Malfec: Ha! Ha! That's funny; you really haven't been listening to me. And you sure as hell don't believe me yet.

Officer Rendell: I believe you need help, you may need psychiatric treatment.

Malfec: Listen to me. I can cure you if you let me. You will have a long life with your children. They have no father do they?

Officer Rendell: He left a long time ago.

Malfec: Then what are you waiting for? To die?

Officer Rendell: You are insane.

Malfec: Get Officer Morris and I will finish my story and tell you about the three thugs that tried to kill me and my brother.

Officer Rendell steps out and returns with Officer Morris.

The camera is on and we are recording your statement. You have been read your rights and you have the right to an attorney. Do you understand?

Malfec: Yes.

Officer Rendell: Good, tell us what happened in the parking lot.

Malfec looks down as he starts. My brother and I were driving back to New Jersey so that I could return him to the group home where he stays.

Officer Morris: Wait a minute, since you decided to yap away would you like to tell us your name for the record.

The name of this host is Dr. Tom Brant. My name is Malfec.

Officer Morris: Aw shit here we go again. OK so you are Dr. Tom Brant. What kind of Doctor?

Malfec: I have a PhD in Computer Science.

Officer Morris: Great a Geek beats up three hoods; do you expect us to believe that?

Malfec: I am glad you realize they were hoods. At least we understand that they were not saints. Should I continue?

Officer Morris: Yeah go ahead.

Malfec: As I was saying we were returning to New Jersey. It was a Sunday afternoon around three pm. I was a little tired from taking care of him for the past three weeks and I was a little burned out from a long week at work. I was travelling east on route 95 and had just crossed the bridge over the Susquehanna River and I noticed a dark car coming up in my rear view mirror. They'd accelerate up to my bumper like they were going to ram me from behind and then back off. They were so close that I could see them laughing in my rear view mirror. As I continued across the bridge toward the Perryville side of Maryland, I thought I would take the next exit to avoid trouble. I was driving my Ford Ranger which isn't a high value car. So when they followed us off the exit I knew they had other intentions than taking my truck. I slowed down so that I could look for help anywhere and hoped that I might spot a police car or some other place that would discourage them from following me and my helpless brother. They bumped my bumper and I could hear them cursing me and calling out names. They were yelling me to pull over you freaking cracker but they didn't say it that way. I am seventy and I guess that made me an easy

85

victim. I was still looking for a way to de-escalate and escape these assholes. No such luck. I pulled into the casino parking lot and felt my bumper get hit harder.

As I drove around the parking lot, it seemed extremely empty for a weekend day but being Sunday I was hoping that there might be more people. I couldn't find a security car or anything. I even drove up to the front door and there were no valets outside. You can view the security tapes and I am sure you'll see me drive by the front entrance. As I drove around the corner of the casino, they hit my car really hard and I jerked forward and I stalled against a car in the parking lot. They ran right up behind me and blocked me from going forward or back. I was cornered. I looked around the lot and there was no one to help as they jumped out of the car. Their car was black and painted with primer, a real junker. I decided I stood a better chance outside the car than inside. As I jumped out the driver side I could smell their stench and I knew they were truly evil. I could smell their putrid souls that surpassed the color of their skin. The driver was short and covered in tattoos but his skin was so dark I couldn't see what they were supposed to represent. I remember thinking how stupid it was for him to get tattoos. He started cursing at me as he lifted up the driver seat to let out the giant in the back seat. I could see the weasel in the passenger seat reach for something under his seat and then slowly get out of the car. He took his time and just stood at the passenger side of the car looking around. The giant in the back was told by the rancid punk driving to kick my ass. He had a baseball bat and ran at me. I kept a monkey wrench under the driver seat to tighten the tow ball on my truck and as he rushed me I swung upward with the two foot long wrench with all my demon power and I damn near took off his head below the jaw. The punk at the driver side of the car was right behind the ape that rushed me and caught me a glancing blow on my arm with a tire iron. I dropped the wrench but swung around so quickly that I was able to send both fingers into his eyes. He fell screaming like a baby and blind. I picked up the tire iron as the passenger side punk approached my brother's side of the truck. I jumped over the hood of the truck and met the punk half way. He had a knife. He was yelling at me and telling me I was going to die and that he was going to ram the tire iron up the other guy's ass, meaning my brother. I reversed the tire iron to the pointy end and lunged full force at the assholes face until I drove the pointy end of the tire iron into his eye and didn't stop until it came out the back of his skull. He dropped like a dead carp and I twisted the tire iron until the top of his head came off.

Meanwhile the leader of this scum was thrashing on the ground. Blood and goo was gushing out of his eyes. I picked up the knife his now deceased buddy was going to use on my brother and decided that I would leave an example for other members of his ilk. I cut off his arms at the shoulder and dragged him by the feet to his piece of junk. I hooked his feet to the bumper, put his car in reverse, and used his arm to push on the accelerator. He flew in reverse across the parking lot as the car finally ran over his worthless stump. As I was returning to my car and my brother, the first ape whose face I nearly tore off was starting to moan or gurgle something. I decided that he wasn't going to give any mercy to me or my brother as nasty as he smelled, so turn about was fair play. Besides my adrenalin was so pumped I thought this body was going to have a heart attack. I stuck the asshole's head under my front tire and backed up. All I saw as I backed out of the parking lot was a headless corpse. All three of these assholes were wearing gang colors so I thought why should I wait around and get jacked up by some of their asshole buddies.

I drove off and as you know I stopped in Wilmington Delaware at the car wash where I was getting the filth off my car and another patron must have copied my license. After I took my brother home and got him settled in I turned on the news and saw the story. The all-points bulletin describing my vehicle and the license left me no choice but to turn myself in. I called the station and was escorted down here by two uniform officers. One of them thanked me for taking out what he called trash. Does that sound about right?

Officer Rendell: You do realize you just confessed to several brutal murders?
Malfec: I just confessed to self-defense and eliminating a bunch of scum that would have terrorized some other poor helpless elderly citizen that you are supposed to protect. Instead you are more concerned about the fact that they were black, instead of the fact that they were criminals that you had let loose on the streets to scare old people. They were white haters and scum, ah, but reverse racism is

ok. How many other people had these three hurt, robbed, possibly killed. The one asshole had two tears tattooed under his right eye. Do you know what that means officer? That means he killed two people. Do you have any unsolved murders of older white people who had their heads crushed in? I know you do because I could smell their deaths on this asshole. I can tell you that one was an elderly lady walking home from the store carrying groceries when she was surrounded by these three innocent youths, as the big fat one whose head I took off clubbed her from behind so hard that her eyes popped out her socket. The short punk with tattoos then kicked her in the throat, killing her. Well, Rendell, do you have that unsolved murder on your murder board?

Behind the glass the desk sergeant was watching the interrogation with the local District Attorney. He looked at the DA and asked how the hell this guy knew about the details of that homicide as no press release was given. The DA looked quizzical and said "I don't care I just got this case wrapped in nice tidy on tape bundle." Get him out of there and put him back in his cell as I tell the press that he confessed.

Chapter Eighteen

The Power of Powers.

As Malfec is escorted to the cell he leans over to the guard. Hey officer, I want to talk to Officer Rendell.

Guard: She went home you'll have to wait until tomorrow.
Malfec: Hey, I'll bet there is a crowd gathering outside.
Guard: There is a hell of crowd outside and they all want to hang you.
Malfec: What about you?
Guard: I don't care what they do to you, now shut up. I want to eat my dinner in peace.
Malfec: When are they going to feed me?
Guard: They'll be somebody coming around in about an hour.
Malfec: Can I get a drink of water?
Guard: I'll be right back.

The guard disappeared and returned within a minute. He put the water on the serving shelf. Then he opened the serving door. Malfec reached out and grabbed the glass and then told the guard to look at the water. The guard leaned forward and could not believe what he saw. The water had turned bronze and had a fragrant smell that the guard knew well. He had been a secret alcoholic for twenty years. The saliva in his mouth started forming and he could taste that sweet taste in his mouth that could only be satisfied by sipping the whiskey that he depended on after work. He needed it to get to sleep and to sleep all night. It was the only thing that stopped the night sweats that started after he came back from Vietnam. It stopped the nightmares. It was a far better solution than the pills the VA gave him. He leaned closer and he smelled the glass again. He was dying to take a sip but it would mean losing his job. It would smell on his breath and in his sweat especially after last night's binge. He could taste it now as well as smelled. He had to have it. He looked up and saw Malfec smiling. After all, this is what demons do. Temptation is mastered but the desire has to exist first. The smell grew stronger and the guard was salivating, his eyes were tearing, his nose was running. He was reaching for the glass. Malfec knew he would drink it but that was not what he wanted to happen. After all, regardless of being cast out he still had his angelic powers and Malfec had been a Power. This meant that besides being one of the most powerful of once angels he also was the one phylum of angel that could heal. He could heal any disease, injury, or non-fatal soul wrenching illness.

Malfec: What would you give to never want a drink again in your life?

Guard: I can't live without drinking. I can't sleep. I have nightmares and cold sweats. I dream that I'll be dead before I wake up. The booze kills all that. I pass out and I wake up. Every day this is what I do. I have no wife, she left. My kids are grown up and they don't call or look in on me. I only have work and booze. That's it.

Malfec: I can't improve your social life but what if I helped you never want a drink in your life again? Would you help me?

Guard: If you think I'll help you break out, your nuts.

Malfec: I only want you to get a message to Officer Rendell as soon as possible.

Guard: That's it. I'd do that anyway. What's the message?

Malfec leans forward and whispers as the guard gasps at the words he hears. The guard staggered back and as he fell back his body jerked and twisted. His eyes rolled up into his head and his mouth opened wide but no noise escaped. Then a voice reverberates through the room in pain. It is not the guard's voice but that of another outcast as his image is shredded and can be heard to scream screw you Malfec.

Guard: Where am I?

Malfec: You are beginning a new life. Please carry my message to Officer Rendell.

Guard: Who is Officer Rendell and who are you?
Malfec: Come here and I'll tell you.

Malfec grabs the dazed guards arm and his memory returns intact. He has actually healed a departing demon's damage. The guard stares at him and thanks him and leaves the area.

Malfec: Well, do you want to drink this?
Guard: Never, never again.

An hour later Officer Rendell appears before Malfec's cell and screams at him.

How the hell did you know I was going to kill myself? That idiot guard you sent to me was babbling about you telling him to tell me not to think about it, that my children need me. They don't need me. Besides I'll be dead in 9 months.

Malfec: No you won't.
Officer Rendell: When did you become a physician?
Malfec: I have always been one.
Officer Rendell: You asshole, you fix computers.
Malfec: This host fixes and masters computers, but I told you what I was and you don't believe me. Even though I am a demon I was once one of the most powerful of angels, in fact we were known as the Powers. We had the power to heal anything except diseases caused by aging. We cannot offer eternal youth. Since being cast out of heaven our powers have not been reduced nor have they gotten stronger, but they are still retained.
Officer Rendell: So go ahead and heal me.

Malfec looked at her. I could but I am offering you an alternative to just being healed. Besides what would it benefit me to have you healed and then have you turn against me and testify that I admitted to you that I had murdered those punks. The black crowd outside is screaming for vengeance and they don't care about the circumstances of the situation.

They just see whitey getting the better of three thugs and that means that it had to be underhanded and the police are covering it up. But I have a plan that resolves everybody's problems.

Officer Rendell: You're a damn demon with a conscience and a sense of justice, bullshit.

Malfec: I can help you and you can help me. What do you have to lose? I told you this host was dying at age ten when I saved him. And now I'm seventy and still alive but this host has been diagnosed with a brain tumor caused by dementia and he will die within the year. Of course he will never suffer as long as I am inside but it has gone too far now and I have to spare his family the pain of the suffering associated with a onetime genius babbling and drooling in his last days.

Officer Rendell: Listen, what makes you think that anything you say makes sense other than the confession you made on tape today.

Malfec: You have to believe that there is more to existence than just living and dying and leaving everyone behind. You must believe in something.

Officer Rendell: I'll tell you what I believe and that it's not having a demon inside me directing all my future actions. I believe that all men lie. If they can they will get over on any woman and abandon them at the first sign of trouble. Just as you have done before with other female hosts you possessed. You want me to turn over control of my mind and body to you so you can escape your situation.

Malfec: It won't be like that. We will share the experience of life and you will know health and clear mindedness. Your children will have a mother and your life will be improved as well as theirs. Think about them without a mother. Can you live with yourself leaving them to fend for themselves in a foster home?

Officer Rendell: My sister will take care of them.

Malfec: Your sister is a pharmaceutical junkie and you know it. So you would let her take care of your three year old daughter? Do you feel good about that? Your kids will be taken away from your sister within three months after she brings them into her dump. You know it. You are in denial. Do you really trust the men she has brought into her house? There have been scum balls in her life that she must have picked up the day after they were let out of prison. Is that the environment you want for your children?

Officer Rendell: Just stop, I can't take this bullshit anymore. You are so full of bull. Why are you doing this to me?

Malfec: OK just think about it and tomorrow we can go back in the interrogation room and talk. Just don't tell anyone else about this.

Officer Rendell leaves crying. As she runs out of the station house one of the street reporters try to ask her a question and sticks a microphone into her face. She grabs the arm of the reporter and twists the arm sending him into the side of his news van. She runs to her car and speeds away.

Chapter Nineteen

Complications

Inside the precinct in front of the Desk Sergeant a tall dark haired man approaches the desk and shows a detectives badge. I'm Detective Madrigal from Homicide and I understand that you have a Doctor Brant here being held for murder.

Desk Sergeant: Yeah he's here.

Detective Madrigal: I need to talk with him.

Desk Sergeant: Sorry, nobody sees him without Officer Rendell present.

Detective Madrigal: Who the hell is Officer Rendell?

Desk Sergeant: She made the collar and has been interrogating him.

Detective Madrigal: I don't care what she was doing but it stops now and I want to see him. Got that?

Desk Sergeant: I'll have him brought to interrogation room 3.

Detective Madrigal: Let me know when he gets there, I'm going to talk to your Captain. We're old friends.

Desk Sergeant: Yes sir. Give me five minutes.

Outside the precinct the crowd is growing. A news camera is set to go from Channel 3 and Nancy Gates the local reporter is having her makeup done as the cameraman gives her the signal for three minutes.

Nancy Gates: Hurry up with the hair, would you. Make sure there isn't a strand out of place.

Cameraman: You are on in three, two, and gives the signal in silence for one.

Nancy Gates: This is Nancy Gates for News Channel three. I am here outside the precinct where Doctor Brant is being held for murder of three youths. The bodies of the three were found dismembered and left outside the Ridge Casino off Route 95 in Maryland. I have with me a friend of one of the three youths that were killed. What's your name?

Youth: Clarence.

Nancy Gates: Did you know the three youths that were killed?

Youth: Yeah that's some shit, they was murdered. The Popo ain't doin nothing, theys jus interested in savin that hunky doc in dare.

Nancy Gates: There are some rumors that your friends were threatening the doctor and he only acted in self-defense. What do you think about that?

Youth: It's bull man, they was probably jus funin with him.

Nancy Gates: What do you mean "funin"?

Youth: You know, just tappin his bumper and laughin.

Nancy Gates: Do they do that often?

Youth: Just sometimes, just to crackers, ya know, just for fun.

Nancy Gates: Do you think running into the back of another person's car is fun?

Youth: Yeah man, we all have to do it, ya know to belong.

Nancy Gates: To belong to what?

Youth: Look at my hat, what color is it? You figure it out.

Nancy Gates looks at his hat as the cameraman zooms in.

He gives some gang hand symbols to the camera and smiles and shows his grill, a mouth full of intricate silver.

Nancy Gates: Are you telling us that this was all the result of some gang initiation?

Youth: No way, these guys were already members; they didn't need to initiate nothing.

Nancy Gates: Thanks Clarence. Let's move over here to the Reverend Pursey. Reverend do you have anything to say about the three supposed gang members that were killed.

Reverend Pursey: Oh so now all black youths are gang members and deserve to get murdered. These three youngsters were just enjoying an afternoon Sunday ride when they were accosted by these two troublemakers looking for an excuse to rile up the community. They were not gangsters.

Youth: Yeah they was. And proud of it.

Nancy Gates: Well what do you say to that Reverend Pursey?

Reverend Pursey: That's typical of the media causing doubt because there's two white men in the jail.

Nancy Gates: Reverend, you do know that one of the two men you are talking about has Downs Syndrome and couldn't harm anyone.

Reverend Pursey: That's nonsense. That's just another excuse to get them out.

Nancy Gates: No it is the truth and the police have already let him go. In fact it has been established that he never left the truck even after the three gang members had rammed them from behind.

Reverend Pursey: Says who, the white police? These were just boys and they were killed.

Nancy Gates: Reverend those boys were twenty one and one was twenty eight, do you still consider them boys?

The camera shifts right as a tall man enters the shot. Detective Madrigal steps into the shot and grabs the microphone. Those were not boys they were animals and they got put down like the dogs they were. For crying out loud, they were going to kill a mentally retarded man for fun. They just picked the wrong person to mess with. I hope it sends a sign to the rest of their friends, right Clarence?

Youth: Detective Mad Dog where did ya come from?

Detective Madrigal: Get lost chump you had your five minute of shame. Miss Gates I am going to ask you to remove your truck from in front of the precinct and move it a block away or I will have it impounded for blocking a city street. Thank you in advance. I have to get back to my interview.

Desk Sergeant: Nice job out there Mad Dog.

Detective Madrigal: Is Doctor Brant in the room now?

Desk Sergeant: He's there and he's all yours. Officer Rendell is on her way in.

Detective Madrigal saunters into the room holding the murder book and eyeballs Dr. Brant. He walks around the chair several times before saying anything. He looked at the murder book that Officer Rendell had put together and looked at the pictures of the three victims. He started shaking his head and looks down occasionally at Dr. Brant but doesn't say anything but keeps reading the book. Finally he lays the book on the table and points to the pictures and says, "How the hell did a wimp like you kick the shit out of these three thugs?"

Malfec looks up at Madrigal.

Malfec: I didn't kick anybody.

Madrigal: So now you are a wise ass.

Malfec: No actually I have a PhD in Computer Science.

Madrigal: So you're a freaking geek too?

Malfec: If that is how you want to characterize me.

Madrigal: Did you feel threatened by these youths?

Malfec: What do you see in those three assholes that would make you call them youths? How would you feel if those three got into your space, cursing, calling you names, and standing right next to you was your ten year old son?

Madrigal: How the hell do you know I have a ten year old boy?

Malfec: Have you not reviewed the recording that I have given for the past two days? Are you really that stupid?

Madrigal: You mean that demon bull shit? What is that some kind of insanity defense you are preparing?

Malfec: It's no defense; in fact I'll never go to trial.

Madrigal: Do you think you are going to walk out the door and never be charged? Do you know what is going on outside these precinct doors? There are people out there that want to lynch you. You better hope you don't get bail because you are safer in here than out there.

Malfec: Those crowds will go away soon. People get tired after a while, especially if they have families. It is only professional dissidents and media freaks that the broadcasting networks pump up that cause normal people to gather in crowds. Every one of those mindless idiots hopes to get on TV to tell their ignorant friends about their 15 seconds of fame.

Madrigal:'So you think they are idiots?

Malfec: They are protesting about a situation that if they were faced with the same event except the three thugs approaching them were white motorcycle gangs members, they would probably be dead and they would be the victims and the same crowd would be out there protesting for the person attacked instead protesting for the attackers.

Madrigal: I see your point and you are probably right – the same people would be out there and they would probably be blaming the police for not being everywhere to save them. Then when we are everywhere they start crying harassment. If you're white you can't win. So are you a bigot?

Malfec: How could I be a bigot? I have been black, yellow, white, and red. If you listened to my statements you would already know that.

Madrigal: Oh Yeah, the insanity defense.

Malfec: It is not a defense, it is a fact. Do you really think that you know everything there is to know about this world you live in? Are you religious?

Madrigal: I go to church.

Malfec: You go to church every Sunday. You are a Catholic and your son goes to Catholic school which is costing you a good amount for a detective. You have read only portions of the bible but you are familiar with the gospel about Jesus casting out demons. Just what did you think that meant when you read it?

Madrigal: I just thought that those people were ill and they were healed.

Malfec: Do you believe in the Devil?

Madrigal: Yeah because I see him every day.

Malfec: What you see are humans succumbing to evil desires, what you think you see is not the devil. If you saw Lucifer you would never recognize his true personage. However if you have some grotesque image that you believe in, he can conjure that up, just like any demon could.

Madrigal: So you are saying that you could make me see you as a demon?

Malfec: Any demon could make you see whatever they wanted but what would be the purpose? Are you so special that you believe that you above all other humans have something special to offer the outcasts from heaven?

Madrigal: Why not, I have a soul, I thought demons wanted souls.

Malfec: And you think we want your soul? Do you know that we have an overabundance of human idiots trying to get into what they think is hell.

Madrigal: What do you mean "they think is hell?"

Malfec: If you knew what hell was like, it would be the last place you would ever want to visit, let alone stay. Why do you think demons fight to possess humans? It's because they want to stay out of hell.

Madrigal: Enough of this shit, it doesn't matter

Malfec: I am trying to help you and everyone on earth find what you sought throughout the ages. Demons and angels are real. We are not figments of your imagination. We exist and when someone like me tries to tell you the truth you don't accept it because you have all been brainwashed by the media into thinking you are what you are and there is nothing but here and now. The frightening thing of all is the realization that if we exist then God exists. There are millions of people on this planet that have spent their entire lives fighting belief in God, especially the God in the bible. If God exists than no one needs their government they only need their churches. The fact that I have said that I am a demon presents a dilemma because if I had said I was an angel after having protected my brother, you could easily lock me up and call me a nut. Ah, a demon, that's another story because deep down people believe in demons. Whether people are willing to believe in physical demons can be written off as a human inclination toward evil. That would make your job easier. There is however one problem.

Madrigal: What would that be Mr. Demon?

Malfec: Once my story or at least some of my story comes out, other demons will have stories to tell as well and sooner or later people will start believing as they see what powers we really have.

Madrigal: So what?

Malfec: Then there will be only one outcome, angels will have to reveal themselves and they can come and go as they please and they don't have to possess anything. Angels have no understanding of human tendencies or needs. With the sweep of a sword they can level an entire city. God gave dominion over demons not humans so humans become irrelevant in pursuit of their mission.

Madrigal: This is crazy, I almost started believing you.

Just then Officer Rendell walks in on the interrogation.

Officer Rendell: What the hell are you doing Mad Dog? This is my suspect. Have you recorded his statements?

Madrigal: No.

Officer Rendell: Get out you bastard, get out. You have no right. This is my case.

Madrigal: Do you really think they are going to let you run with this case with all the press that is involved? Why do you think I am here, they don't want you screwing it up. Oh yeah and let me give you some advice, do not talk to the press at all.

Detective Madrigal leaves the room and closes the door behind him.

Officer Rendell: What did you say to him?

Malfec: Everything I have been telling you that you haven't believed.

Officer Rendell: Don't you realize how insane you sound?

Malfec: You mean because I am telling the truth.

Officer Rendell: Don't be absurd, you are a PhD, you know what you are saying, you know there is no research to justify your statements. How can you, such a learned individual believe what you are saying?

Malfec: Do you believe in UFO's?

Officer Rendell: I believe there is a possibility that there are life forms from other planets that may have the ability to come to this planet.

Malfec: So that is a yes?

Officer Rendell: It is possible.

Malfec: You have never seen a UFO but you believe in there possible existence, so why don't you give me the same benefit of the doubt?

Officer Rendell: Because it is too ridiculous.

Malfec: and how ridiculous is it that I beat up three young hoods and got the best of them. You believe I did it, or do you think my brother with Down syndrome helped me? Or maybe an alien helped me.

Officer Rendell: Don't be ridiculous, you admitted that you killed them.

Malfec: Of course I did because it is true just as the rest of my story is real.

Officer Rendell: If you really want me to believe you'll have to come up with something I can wrap my mind around and prove.

Malfec: What more proof do you want; I gave you the murderer of that old woman. Her name was Mildred Pierce.

Officer Rendell: You could have learned that in here. Cons talk. You could have guessed it for all I know and got lucky.

Malfec: I will give you information on a case your neighboring precinct is working that involves an individual in your jurisdiction. It involves the abduction of a female nursing student. They have some video of the girl being kidnapped in the school parking lot but the film is too grainy to make an ID. The individual that took the girl stalked her. He waited in the parking lot for her to leave her class. He's a smoker. I can smell it. Day to day he appears as a normal hard working individual but when he gets home he turns into a sadistic rapist. The girl is being tortured but she isn't dead yet, but the time is coming when he will tire of this girl and go out and get another.

Officer Rendell: Anyone can offer a profile especially someone as smart as you with access to the internet.

Malfec: Rendell, the individual doing this works in this precinct.

Officer Rendell: What? Who is it? Is it a cop?

Malfec: Nope, first you swear that you will believe everything I have told you if I give up the name.

Officer Rendell: First I need to know how you know.

Malfec: I smelled him when I walked by him. I told you that evil stinks and this guy smells bad.

Officer Rendell: Is it a cop?

Malfec: NO, it is a clerk out front.

Officer Rendell: Who?

Malfec: His name tag read Stanick.

Officer Rendell: Jim Stanick? No way.

Malfec: I told you that day to day he appears normal. You have the name and now what will you do about it.

Officer Rendell: I don't know, I have to think about it.

Malfec: Well you better hurry; I don't think that girl has much time left. He thinks you cops are stupid even though he failed the entrance test to the police academy.

Officer Rendell: That's something I can verify.

Malfec: Don't let him find out you are researching him, he has access to the computer files and I don't think you have the experience to cover your digital tracks.

Officer Rendell: No but you do.

Malfec: That's true.

Officer Rendell: I'm going to take you down to central records and you're going to help me, if you want me to believe you.

Malfec: I can do that.

Officer Rendell steps out of the interrogation room and approaches the desk sergeant to let him know that she is done and bring the prisoner back to his cell.

Once Dr. Brant is back in his cell, Rendell walks into lock up and asks the guard to let him out because the DA wants to question him. Leave the handcuffs on him.

Officer Rendell: Ok come with me.

Malfec: OK

Officer Rendell: Let me do the talking. I'll ask for a research room and tell them that it is part of another case that you may be connected to and I want you to identify online booking images. Once inside the room, you'll only have ten minutes after I pull his file to cover my tracks.

At the computer console, Rendell pulls Stanick's personnel jacket and sure enough the jacket shows that he failed the police academy entrance exam. Rendell quickly writes down the current address of Stanick. She sees that he has no family.

Malfec: OK, I need your password. I am accessing the log and erasing your
search. I have erased your log on and evidence that you signed on.

Officer Rendell: That took you less than a minute.

Malfec: That's how I make a living.

Officer Rendell: OK I have to take you back to the room.

Once back in the interrogation room Malfec asks if the camera is on.
Rendell says it is.

Malfec: Good, then I need to continue and tell you something you need to
know. You have to understand that even humans call us demons
for lack of any other term that will satisfy their understanding
but we were once angels. The fact that we were once angels means
that at our core we were once what you would call good. We cared
about each other, we cared about doing right, and we cared about
He Who Always was. We did not care for humans and most angels
still do not. Ask yourself, which has been more prevalent over
the centuries, the spotting of demons or visits by angels. This is
not a hard question to answer in any century. Where have all the
angels been? Not here. Why? Because they believe that humans
are inherently evil and that they stink. Angels are pure and they
avoid anything that is not pure, namely humans. We, the other
side of angels, have learned to tolerate the smell of normal humans,
especially after spending time in the nowhere which really stinks.
But there are some humans that smell so bad to us that we can
recognize from a distance how really evil they are. They reek of
the evil deeds they have committed. Whenever we come in contact
with one of these humans we can see their evil deeds. We also can
see the reason they have committed such sins. It comes to us like
a fast motion video. The more evil they have committed the longer
the video. When creatures such as these die they go to the nowhere
and become the personal property of Lucifer. They contribute to
the smell of the nowhere and compound the discomfort of being
shredded because there stink is shredded and blasted all over the
nowhere. Occasionally the Light gets a kick out of sending one of
these souls back to earth to possess a human. After being shredded

and then finding themselves back on earth they go crazier than they were the first time. Over time they learn to control and conceal their actions so that they can avoid being shredded again. However, they have little concern for the health of the human and allow the body to deteriorate. Those of us that have been outcast, we actually preserve the health of the human we inhabit. So the bible stories of the Son of He Who Always was casting out demons is a writer's interpretation of the scene. The victims were deteriorating physically. This means that they were being possessed by Lucifer's returned souls. The scene does not depict casting out demons but rotten souls returned to earth for Lucifer's pleasure. The bible story was written as the casting out of demons in the New Testament but this was from a human writer's perspective. Don't get me wrong, we can be cast out of a human as I have already discussed in some of my adventures. The possession by one of us is more of a symbiotic relationship, whereas the possession by a previously dead malefaction is chaotic. It renders the possessed human insane, which is often the diagnosis by modern science, but it is really the free will of the person possessed with the possessing entity ripping their mental capacities until they yield to will of the possessor. I think that this undertaking is despicable and many of us have argued with the Light i.e. Lucifer about these possessions but he keeps saying that there is a purpose to it all.

Many of the outcast angels started questioning Lucifer's intentions when he placed the shredded soul of Wladislau Dragwlya into the body of the wounded and blinded Herr A. Schicklgruber Hiedler nee Hüttler nee Huettier better known as Adolf Hitler. Wladislau Dragwlya has been immortalized in history as Vlad the Impaler due to his favorite method of dispatching his enemies. The family surname Dragwlya was contorted into the word Dracula, the shortened Romanian word drac meaning devil. Indeed he was not the devil but the fact that his evil personality exceeded the bounds of what was considered evil at the time led to his demise. An ally of Vlad was named Corvinus a Hungarian king seeking the papacy. He wanted to be pope so bad that he would betray Eastern Europe and Vlad. This betrayal did not sit well with Vlad's other Eastern Europe allies who knew that he was an avid defender of the church and instilled great fear in the Turks who were devoutly Muslim. Corvinus was fearful of executing Vlad so he ambushed him and kept him in prison. He was freed by seducing and marrying the cousin of Corvinus and the daughter of one Vlad's ally. Later Vlad regained his throne and led a battle against the Turks, he was captured, killed and decapitated. The Turks feared Vlad and wanted to ensure that everyone knew he was dead so it was rumored that they placed his head in honey to preserve it and later put it on display on a stake. He was no better off once he was shredded. He stunk up the nowhere so bad that many of the outcasts begged Lucifer to put him back on earth anywhere. They even asked if Lucifer could find a penguin in Antarctica to put his soul in. Lucifer said no, he was saving him for a special job in the future and that time came on 15 October 1918. A blind and wounded Adolf Hitler lay on a hospital gurney outside the hospital in Pasewalk. The hospital staff left those exposed to mustard gas on gurneys in the street in hopes that the fresh air would help heal the burned eyes of the soldiers. Inside of the hospital was where the more serious wounded were kept that needed attention in order to save their lives. The moaning of the wounded could be heard by those outside who believed that they had been placed outside because they were too serious to be treated and would face death shortly. Hitler felt a minor wound on his head and felt the blood but couldn't see how bad it was. He heard the rustling of many soldiers past his litter but everyone was too busy to pay attention. The shelling of German factories from the allies could be heard. Hitler had been carried to the hospital but was unaware of his location or his true condition. He had witnessed the permanent blindness many of his fellow soldiers experienced when exposed to mustard gas and he was afraid. He was afraid that he was going to die. Everyone but Hitler knew he was on his way to recovery and would only suffer temporary blindness, but if he was told he did not believe it. He felt abandoned. He thought he was meant for greater things in Germany. He was a decorated soldier and war hero. He had ideas on how to reform Germany. He was too young to die. So, when the angel of light approached this Herr Hitler with a deal to save his life and restore him back to health this egomaniac jumped at the deal. Make way for Vlad the Impaler.

As soon as Vlad jumped out of the nowhere into the hell bound Hitler there was no need to hide their merged feelings. They were a nightmare made in hell. Lucifer knew this and laughed at his creation. The rest of us were shocked. I knew who Hitler was because I had been at the Battle of the Somme and between changing sides from the Brits to the Germans and back again, I was present when Hitler was wounded the first time before the exposure to Mustard gas. In fact I shot him in the leg but didn't have time to finish him off when another German soldier started firing a machine gun at my host. He crawled away and I take it that he was taken back to Germany and hospitalized for his wound, but at the time I really didn't care but I smelled him on the battlefield way above the many other soldiers that surrounded me. He was evil to the core and that's why I shot him. I just regret that I didn't kill him because between Lucifer, Vlad, and Adolf the worst atrocities ever practiced on human beings, especially the Jewish people were perpetrated within the next 25 years.

You might ask why the Jewish people were the target of such hatred by Adolf Hitler but you are asking the wrong question. The Jewish people were targeted due to a triad of hatred and circumstance. Hitler did feel that the German Jewish population held all the wealth in Germany to the detriment of non-Jewish Germans. They were heavily involved in the banking and merchant businesses in Germany and continued to accumulate more wealth and power after World War I was over. This natural resentment was fueled by his political interests and he needed a rallying point to generate his political career. Vlad the Impaler felt betrayed by the Jewish people in Israel. During the crusades the Christians were liberating the Holy Land at the cost of many of Vlad's soldiers, friends and countrymen. When the Christians finally took back Jerusalem from the Muslims they were not well received by the Jewish people and none of the Jewish population ever lifted a finger to assist the Christians in achieving their freedom. This lack of gratitude experienced by Vlad left a sour taste towards the Jews by this Eastern Europe Royalty that gave up the comforts of his kingdom to free their land. This was an insult that was not easily forgotten even in the nowhere. Now with his freedom inside of Hitler they collaborated mentally on how to annihilate not just the German Jewish population but the Jewish population of the entire world.

Finally the third leg of the stool, Lucifer had conferred with Vlad in the nowhere on his master plan for Jewish annihilation. Lucifer felt scorned by the Jewish people for ignoring his existence. They do not acknowledge Lucifer as anything except a tendency in humans to give in to evil doings during lapses of good conscious. He wanted them to acknowledge his existence and by bringing these two evil sentient beings together in one personality the only logical conclusion one could reach is that there exists a manifest evil known as Satan. It was Lucifer's egomaniacal predisposition to be known that caused the Jewish people to become the target of his anger. He was losing the last vestiges of his angelic personality. If a demon could be considered insane, he was ten steps beyond that.

Chapter Twenty

I Believe, now what?

Officer Rendell was not completely sure she believed Dr. Brant and thought she was being played, but she couldn't figure out why Dr. Brant would want to take her down this path. When she got home she immediately ran to her computer and typed in the search "Jesus casts out demons." Was this phrase really in the bible, was it ever witnessed by other humans that demons exist. Before she could finish her thoughts up popped on the screen: Matthew 8:28-34 "When He came to the other side into the country of the Gadarenes, two men who were demon-possessed met Him as they were coming out of the tombs. *They were* so extremely violent that no one could pass by that way. ²⁹ And they cried out, saying, "What business do we have with each other, Son of God? Have You come here to torment us before the time?" ³⁰ Now there was a herd of many swine feeding at a distance from them. ³¹ The demons *began* to entreat Him, saying, "If You *are going to* cast us out, send us into the herd of swine." ³² And He said to them, "Go!" And they came out and went into the swine, and the whole herd rushed down the steep bank into the sea and perished in the waters. ³³ The herdsmen ran away, and went to the city and reported everything, including what had happened to the demoniacs. ³⁴ And behold, the whole city came out to meet Jesus; and when they saw Him, they implored Him to leave their region."

She continued her search for other references and there were so many that she could not keep count. Then she clicked on Mark 7:25-30 and read "But immediately a woman whose little daughter had an unclean spirit heard of him and came and fell down at his feet. Now the woman was a

Gentile, a Syrophoenician by birth. And she begged him to cast the demon out of her daughter. And he said to her, "Let the children be fed first, for it is not right to take the children's bread and throw it to the dogs." But she answered him, "Yes, Lord; yet even the dogs under the table eat the children's crumbs." And he said to her, "For this statement you may go your way; the demon has left your daughter." She read it again, and realized that these were Jesus's words not Mark's words. Mark was repeating what Jesus said. There were demons in the world and now she was almost positive. What would be her next step. She didn't want to die. She had to see if Jim Stanick was guilty of what Dr. Brant told her. It was time for her to do a little investigation on her own.

Back at the precinct the next morning:

Officer Morris: Sarge, what are you going to do about that crowd out front they are blocking the entrance to our parking.

Desk Sergeant: So where did you park?

Officer Morris: In your space, I saw your wife drop you off.

Desk Sergeant: Morris, you are an asshole.

Officer Morris: Sure I am, can I have the interrogation room to question Brant some more.

Desk Sergeant: Aren't you going to wait for Rendell?

Officer Morris: What for?

Desk Sergeant: Duh! She has the lead on this. You know what Morris, as soon as she gets in, I'll let you know and the two of you can question him.

Officer Morris: Fine! I'll go back into the tombs and question him there.

What a beautiful morning desk sergeant.

Says who?

I'm agent Brisbo and this is my partner agent Jeffers.

So, what can I do for you other than look at your credentials?

Very well, here they are. As both agents whipped out NSA credentials identifying them as special agents for the Department of Defense.

Again, what can I do for you special agents?

Brisbo: We are here to take the prisoner Dr. Brant off your hands.

Sergeant: Really, do you think you are doing us a favor?

Brisbo: Well, actually looking at the crowd outside I would have to say we are indeed doing you a favor.

Sergeant: And what makes you think we will just hand over the good doctor to you.

Brisbo: Let's just say that it is a matter of national security.

Sergeant: And what kind of security will it be called when the crowd outside sees you take Doctor Brant out of here?

Brisbo: Don't worry we'll generate a story for you to give to the press.

Sergeant: And you think the district attorney and the arresting officers will buy into that?

Brisbo: That's a local problem Sarge, I'm sure you know how to handle that.

Sergeant: You're right I do, so just stand right there while I bring the Captain down here to meet you.

Brisbo: We have paperwork and don't think that's necessary.

Sergeant: And will you pay my retirement when I am canned?

Brisbo: Really Sergeant, you are exaggerating, don't make a big thing out this.

Sergeant: I won't, I'll let the Captain do that for me.

As the desk sergeant picks up the phone to call the Captain, Agent Brisbo grabs his hand. The desk sergeant with more emphasis than is needed slams the hand down on the desk and pins the agent's hand making Brisbo grimace in pain. Brisbo pulls his hand away and says go ahead and call we'll wait over there.

Captain Jameson enters the booking room and passes by the desk sergeant's parapet.

Jameson: I'm Captain Jameson gentlemen, can I see you credentials.

Brisbo: Captain we are with the Department of Defense and Doctor Brant presents a national security risk. We need to mitigate that risk before he makes any statements in public that might endanger the safety of the country.

Jameson: As I understand it, Doctor Brant is just a computer analyst, Eighty percent of the general public wouldn't know what he was talking about anyway, and the few that would glean anything from his statements if threatening, you would have alternative protocols to mitigate those. Am I correct?

Brisbo: Not exactly, Doctor Brant worked on some very sensitive projects. Projects that even the public would define as disturbing. We need to take Doctor Brant somewhere where his statements will fall on deaf ears.

Jameson: And we need to resolve a triple homicide.

Brisbo: Did you charge him with homicide or are you still probing?

Jameson: Not yet but we are getting very close to an admission.

Brisbo: Let me enlighten you Captain, he wants you to be his soap box so he can reveal very very sensitive issues.

Jameson: As I understand it, at present he speaking about past lives that he believes he lived. I think he's trying to mount an insanity defense.

Brisbo looks at Jeffers concerned but quickly looks away.

Brisbo: Captain Jameson, if he is teetering on losing his mind, it is critical that none of his statements leak out to the public. He possesses a clearance way above the average government individual. He has been involved in projects that need protection. We need to take him away to day.

Jameson: Gentlemen that is not going to happen, but I will introduce you to the interrogating officers and ask if you can monitor the interrogation.

Brisbo: When will they be available?

Jameson: In about an hour, you are welcome to wait here or come back later.

Brisbo: We'll be back in an hour.

As Jameson walks out he leans over to the desk sergeant and says, "Get Rendell down here now."

The phone rings and Rendell answers "Officer Rendell, can I help you?"

"Yes Sergeant, I'll be there in two hours." "Why do you need me in right now?"

"The Captain wants me to what?"

"OK. I'll be there"

Rendell turns to her sister and looks at her condition. She can tell that her little sister is high but she has no choice she has to go into the precinct. "Sandra, can you get your shit together enough to watch the girls. I need to know that they'll be alright if I leave them with you." "Are you high?" Naw, I'm just a little tired.

Rendell: Well stay the hell awake while I'm gone. I shouldn't be that long. You got it?

Sandra: Do you have anything to eat in the house?

Rendell: There's left over pasta in the frig. Heat it up and give it to the girls too. I'll bring home a pizza, just stay awake.

Sandra: Just go, I have it under control.

Rendell: You mess up and I'll kill you. No guests over, you hear?

Sandra: Yeah. Yeah.

Rendell retrieves her service revolver from the hallway closet, checks it, holsters it and goes out the front door. She reaches for car keys and beeps the car. The alarm goes off and she curses under her breadth as she frantically tries to get the alarm to stop. Sandra comes to the front door and yells "What's going on?" Nothing just get back inside and lock the door. Rendell drives down the block wondering what the hell she is going to do to stop the feds from taking Brant.

As Rendell pulls into the precinct parking lot she sees a government car with two males sitting in it. Rendell stays out of sight of the two in the car and takes the back door into the precinct. She sees the Desk Sergeant and nods to him as she ducks into the locker room.

Sergeant: Rendell get out here.

Rendell: Coming.

Sergeant: Let's go in the back.

Rendell follows and says that she is ready to brief the feds.

Sergeant: First, these guys are not Feds, they don't act like real feds. I think this is a DOD assignment outside normal procedure. In some ways

I think these guys are more dangerous than the feds. These guys have that DOD look. The one that says "can do at any cost." I am pretty sure they are ex-military possibly Delta Force.

Rendell: So what are our marching orders? Should we just give Brant up?

Sergeant: Not without official paperwork which these guys didn't have. Jameson talked to them and he is adamant that Brant is staying right here. However, I don't think that the Captain saw what I saw in these guys' eyes. They are not going away without Brant alive or dead, and preferably dead. You need to find out why these guys want Brant so bad and the only way to do that is to ask him.

Rendell: Do you think he'll tell me?

Sergeant: If he doesn't we may have a hard time protecting him.

Rendell: OK, I'm going to see him, please stall these guys if they come in again. They are sitting outside in their car.

Sergeant: I know, I have a guy watching them.

Rendell: Thanks.

Sergeant: Go find out what's going on.

Rendell: I will.

Sergeant: Give me a signal when you have the full story.

Rendell: I'll call the front desk on my cell

Officer Morris walks back to the holding cells. Well, well, Dr. Brant how are we doing today? Are you ready to tell us some more stories? I am just ready to listen with all ears.

Malfec: Listen Morris, you know I won't talk to you without Rendell present. I also know she isn't here.

Officer Morris: So how do you know that?

Malfec: You know I know so quit screwing around.

Officer Morris: Are you sure you know what you are doing?

Malfec: Why are you asking?

Officer Morris: You know why I am asking, you are jeopardizing your defense, and do you really think anyone would believe all this bullshit you are throwing out.

Malfec: I don't know Morris, you tell me, and do you believe it?

Officer Morris: I don't care what you do, it is your problem, but there may be a lot people that might want to have you killed if you continue with this bullshit story.

Malfec: Let me see, do you want me to cry for a lawyer? That would shut me up real quick. Look I want Rendell here; I need to tell her more.

Officer Morris: Yeah, well I don't know where she is. When she gets here I'll let you know.

As he turns to leave Rendell is coming down the hallway.

Officer Rendell: Morris what the hell do you think you are doing.

Officer Morris: Just advising Dr. Brant here of his options.

Officer Rendell: What options?

Officer Morris: You know, I was saying that he has the right to remain silent et cetera et cetera.

Officer Rendell: Dr. Brant has already been informed of his rights, he's a very smart man, I am sure he doesn't need your dimwitted advice.

Officer Morris: Yeah! And you are so bright, let me see, you got knocked up by a guy you don't know, the first man in your life left, you're going to night school to be what, a makeup artist? So who's the dimwit?

Officer Rendell: You sound like you want him to ask for a lawyer.

Officer Morris: Yeah, I do, and then we won't have to deal with the asshole.

Officer Rendell: It's our case, we need to break it. Besides, the feds want to take him away.

Officer Morris: Look at him. He's making jerks out of us.

Malfec: That's not hard in your case Morris.

Officer Morris: I could kill you right now and no one would care, especially not those assholes outside. They would probably give me a medal.

Officer Rendell: Shut up Morris, let's take him to the interrogation room.

As she puts the cuffs on Dr. Brant, he flexes his muscles really tight. They let him out of his cell and they escort him toward the interrogation room.

Rendell: Morris what are you doing, I told you to leave?

Morris: I'm protecting our prisoner; Sarge let me in on the Feds trying to take Brant here so I was trying to find out why he was so valuable to the government that they wanted to spring him.

Rendell: I told you not to speak with him unless I was present.

Morris: Back off Rendell, things have changed.

Rendell: Dr. Brant why do the feds want to take you?

Malfec: Don't know but I do hold a top secret clearance. However, I really don't think they are feds in the sense that you think.

Rendell: Then why would they put you on a list that made the DOD send two goons down here to extract you?

Malfec: You really haven't been listening to what I have been telling you have you?

Rendell: All that demon shit?

Malfec: Exactly.

Rendell: And you think the government has bought into that bullshit.

Malfec: Not the government but people in the government that really don't want the world knowing the truth about our existence.

Rendell: Aw come on.

Malfec: Regardless of what you think, there is no more time to discuss this. Have you thought about what I offered you?

Rendell: I can't, I just don't believe.

Malfec: What have you got to lose? You just have to agree and everything is taken care of.

Rendell: Again, How will I feel, what do I have to do? I'm afraid.

Malfec: You should be more afraid of dying from cancer.

Rendell: I am but at least I know what to expect.

Malfec: Pain – great pain and your children suffering. How was your sister when you left this morning? Was she coherent, alert, and normal?

Rendell: How did you know?

Malfec: I told you what I am and that is what you can become, but the minute those two agents get access to me all bets are off.

Rendell: Why?

Malfec: Rendell, they work for the government but they also work for the Light. They want to stop me from telling my story.

Rendell: Yeah right.

Malfec: Listen to me; they do not want to draw attention to themselves. The stories I told you are all historically true. They can be verified. These guys know that and they want to stop it. I can tell many more events but not if these send me back to be shredded. They know me and they know I am here, and Lucifer is just waiting to get me under his control again and I will never be let out of the nowhere but there is still so much more to my story that needs to be told. No one has ever broken this silence but many have secretly desired for the truth to get out.

Rendell: I think I better move you to the interrogation room. It will be safer in there and can be locked from the inside.

Malfec: If it helps, let's go.

As Malfec walks down the hall toward the interrogation he senses that presence of the two agents at the front desk. He turns to Officer Rendell. She is oblivious to her surroundings. He grabs her shoulder and says "I need your decision."

Rendell: So you think I'll be your free ride out of here and what do you think these agents will do if I take you up on this deal. They'll kill me or worse.

Malfec: They won't know. There is so much of my essence in Doctor Brant they will never detect a new host. My essence after fifty some years has grown so strong there will be nothing they will sense but me.

Rendell: and how will you switch, will I feel pain, I just don't know.

Malfec: We have no more time left.

Rendell: Come on get to the room.

Outside sitting in their bureau car the two DOD agents are growing impatient.

Jeffers says to Brisbo, "what if they won't release him?"

Brisbo: We have our orders.

Jeffers: Which ones?

Brisbo: Don't be a dumbass. We only answer to one authority and we always follow his orders.

Jeffers: I am not going back there without grabbing or killing Brant.

Brisbo: And neither am I.

As Rendell walks Dr. Brant to the interrogation room the Desk Sergeant shakes his head. He's back at his desk and hears the commotion before he sees it. The crowd from outside is pushing their way into the precinct front door led by the good Reverend Pursey yelling for "justice now."

Raising his booming voice above the noise the Sergeant yells to the crowd to calm down. If you behave yourselves I will take a formal complaint from each one of you as I prepare you for your arrest. The crowd pauses while they try to understand what the Sergeant said. Suddenly from all sides blue uniforms surround the crowd forming a gauntlet that leads directly to the Sergeant. As the Sergeant grabs the closest protester he yells again "You're first. What's your complaint?" The protested looks scared as this wasn't what he was expecting to happen. "Speak up, you want justice, State your complaint, NOW" The protester shaken, wriggles free from the sarge's grip and tries to make his way toward the door, but a uniformed police officer heads him off and steers him to a seat at a desk and sits him down. The Sarge gets the next protester in line and grabs him and again yells "State your complaint." The protester looks at the reverend for support, but the Sarge draws his attention back to him and Yells "Well?" again the protester tries to head for the door and another uniformed officer grabs him and puts him in a chair next to a desk. As the other protesters see what is happening those closest to the door start backing out before they get too close to the front of the crowd. As a mass exodus ensues only the reverend remains in front of the Sarge. The reverend is flabbergasted as the crowd heads down the street away from the station.

Reverend: We will not tolerate this kind of intimidation.

Sergeant: Are you ready to file a complaint?

Reverend: This is an outrage.

Sergeant: Is that a crime. I am not familiar with that law.

Reverend: Don't mock me. I will talk to the city council and we will address this outrage.

Sergeant: You go right ahead reverend, talk talk talk we have work to do and you are clogging up my precinct. Would you like to take those bozos over there with you?

Reverend: The council will hear about this. This is a personal assault on our rights.

Sergeant: Just remember reverend that unlawful assembly is a real crime and if you gather outside my precinct one more time, I will you have you arrested. Now take those two with you and get out of my face.

As the reverend turns to exit a uniformed officer is bringing in a red headed female on suspicion of prostitution. The reverend almost crashes into the woman as he turns rapidly to exit. As he collides the woman obviously recognizing the reverend blurts out "Reverend honey, I don't think I'll be able to make our three o'clock session baby." The reverend is stunned and embarrassed as the entire gathering of uniformed police burst out laughing. The hooker looks around and says "What?" as she straightens her red wig.

As Malfec enters the interrogation room he sees the two NSA agents pushing past the front desk and knows who they are. It is Magra and Tenin. Magra is a Throne, a warrior. He can terminate Dr. Brant without hesitation. Magra's claim to fame was the possession of Nathuram Godse. This person was a nobody going nowhere but Magra transformed him into a political activist in India in his late teens. He welcomed Magra as he struggled with gender identity. His parents had raised him as a girl making him easy prey to someone like Magra. Magra influenced his every move and eventually screwed with his beliefs so bad that he became the infamous murderer of Mahatma Ghandi. He was executed a year later but Magra was gone by then leaving Nathuram to rot in an Indian cell until he was hanged. Magra started to pick up his pace to get to Dr. Brant before he was locked inside the interrogation room. He sensed that something was not right but he didn't know what. Tenin was close behind Magra but he was holding off the Desk Sergeant.

Rendell: Morris lock the door; don't let them in.

Morris: What are you talking about. Let who in?

Rendell: Start the recorders.

Rendell gets on the phone and quick dials the district attorney. Look I don't have much time the feds are here and they are trying to take Dr. Brant into their custody for National Security reasons but they don't have any paperwork. What the hell do you mean, give him to them. Are you insane, he's our case? Who got to you? We're keeping him.

Magra started to bang on the door.

Malfec: Are we being recorded.

Officer Rendell: Yes.

Malfec: Did you go out to Stanick's house?

Officer Rendell: No, but I passed on my suspicion to a friend of mine and he went out there. It was as you said.

Officer Morris: What is this all about?

Malfec: You'll see.

Officer Rendell: It's another case that has nothing to do with this.

Officer Morris: What the hell, are you moonlighting?

Officer Rendell: Later, I'll tell you later.

Malfec: Tell him now so the asshole knows what you were doing.

Officer Rendell: It's not important, I'm ready.

Malfec: Thank you.

Officer Rendell: What is wrong with you?

Malfec: Turning red, with his eyes enlarging, his teeth looked as if to grow. His upper body became enlarged and grotesque and his face became distorted as he screamed at Rendell "Now you can believe."

Rendell started to back away from Brant as Morris runs from the room and sees Agent Brisbo drawing his gun. Morris grabs the Glock from Brisbo and clicks off the safety. Brant breaks the cuffs with almost inhuman strength and grabs the sides of Rendell's head and begins to squeeze as he lowers his head to Rendell's face. Brisbo and Morris are struggling for control of the gun. Malfec knows this is on tape and pulls Rendell forcefully toward him as Morris gaining control of the gun turns into the room lowers the gun and fires once. The shot hits Brant in the side of the head and exits the other side as his brain matter is spread across the opposite wall. His hands gripping either side of Rendell's head lets go. He jerks sideways as Morris lunges forward to pull Rendell away. Rendell falls backward dazed from the shock and the sound of the glock going off in the enclosed room. She falls to the floor and looks as Brant's body hits the floor with only half his head intact. Morris grabs Rendell by the arm and lifts her off the ground. The Desk Sergeant is in the door way pushing Brisbo out of the way as Morris is trying to pull Rendell from the room. Other officers are running to the room weapons drawn. Brant's body is on the floor twitching as Morris hears a gasping "Where am I?" leave Brant's lips. Brisbo and Jeffers quickly exit the precinct.

Desk Sergeant: Rendell are you ok?
Officer Rendell: Groggily, I'm ok, I need a drink of water.
Officer Morris: Let me take her to the lounge.
Desk Sergeant: OK I'll call the coroner, give me your gun.

Morris hands over the gun and says it's not his it's that feds gun. He pulled it and I got it away in time to save Rendell. He walks Rendell to the lounge.

Officer Rendell: I want to go home.
Officer Morris: You fool, do you think for a minute I don't know what you did? Did you really think you could put one over on me? Come on, admit it, you're in there?
Officer Rendell: Morris I don't know what the hell you are talking about? I'm leaving. As she stood she walked passed Morris toward the door. Without looking at Morris she said in a very low voice. "good night, Jasper."

Chapter Twenty-One

Epilogue

When Rendell got home she felt renewed. She had a Doctor's appointment tomorrow but she already knew what the outcome would be. Her children met her at the door when she got home and they were sitting on her lap. She was crying but she knew what she had to do next. She put the children to sleep for a nap and she walked into her kitchen and turned on her laptop and tuned the television to a baseball game. The computer screen turned blue and she clicked on the word processor. She created a blank page and centered the cursor. She started typing. MALFEC: A DEMON AUTOBIOGRAPHY.

Printed in the United States
By Bookmasters